Adventure Stories for Eight Year Olds

Helen Paiba is known as one of the most committed, knowledgeable and acclaimed children's booksellers in Britain. For more than twenty years she owned and ran the Children's Bookshop in Muswell Hill, London, which under her guidance gained a superb reputation for its range of children's books and for the advice available to its customers.

Helen was involved with the Booksellers Association for many years and served on both its Children's Bookselling Group and the Trade Practices Committee. In 1995 she was given honorary life membership of the Booksellers Association of Great Britain and Ireland in recognition of her outstanding services to the association and to the book trade. In the same year the Children's Book Circle (sponsored by Books for Children) honoured her with the Eleanor Farjeon Award, given for distinguished service to the world of children's books.

She retired in 1995 and now lives in London.

Adventure

STORIES

for Eight Year Olds

COMPILED BY HELEN PAIBA

ILLUSTRATED BY KERSTIN MEYER

MACMILLAN
CHILDREN'S BOOKS

For Shlomit and Eliav with love HP

First published 2001 by Macmillan Children's Books
a division of Pan Macmillan Limited
20 New Wharf Road, London N1 9RR
Basingstoke and Oxford
www.panmacmillan.com

Associated companies throughout the world

ISBN 0 330 39140 2

5 7 9 8 6 4

A CIP catalogue record for this book is available from
the British Library.

Typeset by SX Composing DTP, Rayleigh, Essex
Printed and bound in Great Britain by
Mackays of Chatham plc, Kent

Contents

The Parrot Pirate Princess

Joan Aiken

The King and Queen were quarrelling fiercely over what the baby Princess was to be called when the fairy Grisel dropped in. Grisel, that is to say, did not drop in – to be more accurate, she popped out of one of the vases on the mantelpiece, looked round, saw the baby and said:

"What's this?"

"Oh, good afternoon," said the King uncomfortably.

"We were just putting you on the list of people to be invited to the christening," said the Queen, hastily doing so. She had presence of mind.

1

"Mmmmm," said Grisel. "Is it a boy or a girl?"

"It's a girl, and the sweetest little—"

"*I'm* the best judge of that," interrupted the fairy, and she hooked the baby out of its satin cradle. "Well, let's have a look at you."

The baby was a calm creature, and did not, as the Queen had dreaded, burst into loud shrieks at the sight of Grisel's wizened old face. She merely cooed.

"Well, you can't say she's very handsome, can you? Takes too much after both of you," Grisel said cheerfully. The baby laughed. "What are you going to call her?"

"We were just wondering when you came in," the Queen said despairingly. She knew that Grisel had a fondness for suggesting impossible names, and then being extremely angry if the suggestions were not taken. Worse – she might want the baby called after herself.

"Then I'll tell you what," said Grisel, eagerly leaning forward. "Call it—"

But here she was interrupted, for the baby, which she still held, hit her a fearful whack on the front teeth with her heavy silver rattle.

There was a terrible scene. The King and Queen were far too well-bred to laugh, but they looked as if they would have liked to. The Queen snatched the baby from Grisel, who was stamping up and down the room, pale with rage, and using the most unladylike language.

"That's right – laugh when I've had the best part of my teeth knocked down my throat," she snarled. "And as for you, you—" She turned to the baby, who was chuckling in the Queen's arms.

"Goo goo," the baby replied affably.

"Goo goo, indeed. I'll teach you to repeat what I say," the fairy said furiously. And before the horrified Queen could make a move, the baby had turned into a large grey parrot and flown out of the window.

Grisel smiled maliciously round the room and said: "You can take me off the christening list now."

She went, leaving the King and Queen silent.

The parrot turned naturally to the south,

3

hunting for an island with palm trees, or at least a couple of coconuts to eat. After some time she came to the sea. She was disconcerted. She did not feel that she could face flying all the way over that cold grey-looking water to find an island that would suit her. So she sat down on the edge to think. The edge where she sat happened to be a quay, and presently a sailor came along, said, "Hello, a parrot," and picked her up.

She did not struggle. She looked up at him and said in a hoarse, rasping voice, "Hello, a parrot."

The sailor was delighted. He took her on board his ship, which sailed that evening for the South Seas.

This was no ordinary ship. It was owned by the most terrible pirate then in business, who frightened all the ships off the seas. And so fairly soon the parrot saw some surprising things.

The pirates were quite kind to her. They called her Jake, and took a lot of interest in her education. She was a quick learner, and before the end of the voyage she knew the most shocking collection of swear words and nautical phrases that ever a parrot spoke. She also knew all about walking the plank and the effects of rum. When the pirates had captured a particularly fine ship, they would all drink gallons of rum and make her drink it too, whereupon the undignified old fowl would lurch about all over the deck and in the rigging, singing, *"Fifteen men on a dead man's chest, Yo ho, ho and a bottle of rum,"* and the pirates would shout with laughter.

One day they arrived at the island where they kept their treasure, and it was all unloaded and rowed ashore. It took them two days to bury it, and the parrot sat by, thinking: "Shiver my timbers, but I'd like to get away and live on this island!" But she could not, for one of the pirates had thoughtfully tied her by the ankle to a tree. She sat swearing under her breath and trying to gnaw through the rope, but it was too thick.

Luck, however, was with her. The second day after they had left the island, a great storm sprang up, and the pirates' ship was wrecked.

"Brimstone and botheration and mercy me!" chorused the pirates, clinging frantically to the rigging. They had little time for more, because with a frightful roar the ship went to the bottom, leaving Jake bobbing about on the waves like a cork.

"Swelp me," she remarked, rose up and flew with the wind, which took her straight back to the island.

"Well, blow me down," she said when she got there. "This is a bit better than living on biscuit among all those unrefined characters.

Bananas and mangoes, bless my old soul! This is the life for me."

She lived on the island for some time, and became very friendly with a handsome grey gentleman parrot already there, called Bill. Bill seemed to know as much about pirates as she did, but he was always rather silent about his past life, so she gathered that he did not want it mentioned. They got on extremely well, however, and lived on the island for about twenty years, which did not change them in the least, as parrots are notoriously long-lived.

Then one day, as they were sharing a bunch of bananas, a frightful hurricane suddenly arose, and blew them, still clutching the bananas, out to sea.

"Hold on tight!" shrieked Bill in her ear.

"I am holding on," she squawked back. "Lumme, Bill, you do look a sight. Just like a pin-cushion!"

The wretched Bill was being fluffed out by the wind until his tail-feathers stood straight up. "Well, you're not so pretty yourself," he said indignantly, screwing his head round to

7

look at her. "Don't half look silly, going along backwards like that."

"Can't you see, you perishing son of a sea-cook," squawked Jake, "it stops the wind blowing your feathers out – have a try."

"It makes me feel funny," complained Bill, and he went back to his former position, still keeping a tight hold on the bananas.

"Mountains ahead – look out!" he howled, a moment or two later. They were being swept down at a terrific speed towards a range of hills.

"Is it the mainland?" asked Jake, swivelling round to get a glimpse. "Doesn't the wind make you giddy?"

"Yes. It's the mainland, I reckon," said Bill. "There's houses down there. Oh, splice my mainbrace, we're going to crash into them. Keep behind the bananas." Using the great bunch as a screen, they hurtled downwards.

"Mind last week's washing," screamed Jake, as they went through a low belt of grey cloud. "I never in all my life saw anything to beat this. Talk about seeing the world." They were only twenty feet above ground now, still

skimming along, getting lower all the time.

"Strikes me we'd better sit on the bananas if we don't want our tail feathers rubbed off," said Jake. "Oh my, look where we're going."

Before Bill had time to answer, they went smack through an immense glass window, shot across a room, breaking three vases on the way, and came to rest on a mantlepiece, still mixed up with the bananas, which were rather squashed and full of broken glass.

"Journey's end," said Jake. "How are you, Bill?"

"Not so bad," said Bill, wriggling free of the bananas and beginning to put his feathers to rights.

Then they were both suddenly aware of the fairy Grisel, sitting in one corner of the room where she had been knocked by a vase, and glaring at them. She picked herself up and came and looked at them closely.

"It's you again, is it?" she said. "I might have known it."

"Pleased to meet you," said Jake, who had no recollection of her. "I'm Jake, and this is my husband Bill."

"I know you, don't you worry," said Grisel. Then Jake suddenly remembered where she had seen Grisel before.

"Oh lor – don't you go changing me into a princess again," she cried in alarm, but hardly were the words out of her beak when, bang, she was back in her father's palace, in the throne-room. She looked down at herself, and saw that she was human once more.

"Well! Here's a rum do," she said aloud. "Who'd have thought it?" She glanced round the room and saw, through a French window, the King and Queen, a good deal older, having tea on the terrace. There was also a girl, not unlike herself. She went forward to them with a nautical gait, and hitching up her trousers – only it was a long and flowing cloth-of-gold skirt.

"Hello, Pa! Pleased to meet you!" she cried, slapping the King on the back. "Shiver my timbers, Ma, it's a long time since we met. Not since I was no longer than a marlin spike. Who's this?"

They were all dumfounded to speak. "Hasn't anyone got a tongue in their head?"

11

she asked. "Here comes the prodigal daughter, and all they can do is sit and gawp!"

"Are you – are you that baby?" the Queen asked faintly. "The one that got taken away?"

"That's me!" Jake told her cheerfully. "Twenty years a parrot, and just when I'm beginning to enjoy life, back I comes to the bosom of my family. Shunt my backstay, it's a funny life."

She sighed.

The King and Queen looked at one another in growing horror.

"And this'll be my little sissy, if I'm not mistaken," said Jake meditatively. "Quite a big girl, aren't you, ducks? If you'll excuse me, folks, I'm a bit thirsty. Haven't had a drink for forty-eight hours."

She rolled indoors again.

"Well, I suppose it might be worse," said the Queen doubtfully, in the horrified silence. "We can *train* her, can't we? I suppose she'll have to be the heir?"

"I'm afraid so," said the king. "I hope she'll take her position seriously."

"And what happens to *me*?" demanded the

younger sister shrilly.

The King sighed.

During the next two months the royal family had an uncomfortable time. Jake obviously meant well, and was kindly disposed to everyone, but she did make a bad Crown Princess. Her language was dreadful, and she never seemed to remember not to say "Stap my vitals" or something equally unsuitable, when she trod on her skirt. She said that trains were a nuisance.

"You don't want to traipse round with the drawing-room curtains *and* the dining-room tablecloth pinned to your tail. I'm used to flying. Splice my mainbrace!" she would cry.

She rushed about and was apt to clap important court officials and ambassadors on the back and cry, "Hello! How's the missus, you old son of a gun?" Or if they annoyed her, she loosed such a flood of epithets on them ("You lily-livered, cross-eyed, flop-eared son of a sea-cook") that the whole Court fled in horror, stopping their ears. She distressed the King and Queen by climbing trees, or sitting rocking backwards and forwards for hours at a time, murmuring, "Pretty Poll. Pretty Jake. Pieces of eight, pieces of eight, pieces of eight."

"Will she *ever* turn into a presentable Queen?" said the King despairingly, and the Queen stared hopelessly out of the window.

"Perhaps she'll marry and settle down," she suggested, and so they advertised for princes in the *Monarchy's Marriage Mart*, a very respectable paper.

"We'll have to think of Miranda too," the King said. "After all, she was brought up to expect to be Queen. It's only fair that she should marry some eligible young Prince and come into a kingdom that way. She's a good girl."

Eventually a Prince arrived. He came quite quietly, riding on a fiery black horse, and stayed at an inn near the Palace. He sent the King a note, saying that he would be only too grateful for a sight of the Princess, whenever it was convenient.

"Now, we must really try and make her behave presentably for once," said the Queen, but there was not much hope in her voice.

A grand ball was arranged, and the Court

dressmakers spent an entire week fitting Jake to a white satin dress, and Miranda obligingly spent a whole evening picking roses in the garden to put in Jake's suspiciously scarlet hair.

Finally the evening came. The throne-room was a blaze of candlelight. The King and Queen sat on the two thrones, and below them on the steps, uncomfortably but gracefully posed, were the two Princesses. A trumpet blew, and the Prince entered. The crowd stood back, and he walked forward and bowed very low before the thrones. Then he kissed Miranda's hand and said:

"Will you dance with me, Princess?"

"Hey, young man," interrupted the King, "you've made a mistake. It's the other one who's the Crown Princess."

Jake roared with laughter, but the Prince had gone very pale, and Miranda was scarlet.

"I didn't know *you* were the Prince of Sitania," she said.

"*Aren't* you the Princess, then?" he said.

"Have you two met before?" the King demanded.

15

"Last night in the Palace gardens," said Miranda.

"The Prince promised he'd dance the first dance with me. But I didn't know, truly I didn't, that he was *that* Prince."

"And I thought you were the Crown Princess," he said. There was an uncomfortable silence. Jake turned away and began humming, "*Yo ho ho and a bottle of rum.*"

"Your Majesty, I am sorry to be so inconvenient," said the Prince desperately, "but may I marry *this* Princess?"

"How large is your kingdom?" asked the King sharply.

"Well, er, actually I am the youngest of five sons, so I have no kingdom," the Prince told him, "but my income is pretty large."

The King shook his head. "Won't do, Miranda must have a kingdom. I'm afraid, young man, that it's impossible. If you wanted to marry the other Princess and help reign over this kingdom, that would be different."

The Prince hung his head, and Miranda bit her lip. Jake tried to put her hands in her white satin pockets, and whistled. The crowd began to shuffle, and to quiet them the Royal Band struck up. And then Jake gave a shriek of delight, and fairly skated across the marble floor.

"*Bill*, my old hero! I'd know you anywhere!" A burly pirate with a hooked nose and scarlet hair was standing in the doorway.

"Well, well, well!" he roared. "Looks like I've bumped into a party. You and I, ducks, will show them how the hornpipe ought to be danced." And solemnly before the frozen Court they broke into a hornpipe, slow at first, and then faster and faster. Finally they stopped, panting.

"I'm all of a lather. Haven't got a wipe, have you, Jake?" Bill asked.

"Here, have half the tablecloth." She tore a generous half from her twelve-foot train and gave it to him. They both mopped their brows vigorously. Then Jake took Bill across to where the King and Queen were standing with horror-struck faces.

"Here's my husband," said Jake. The Court turned as one man and fled, leaving the vast room empty but for the King and Queen, Jake and Bill, and Miranda and the Prince.

"Your husband? But you never said any-thing about him. And here we were, searching for Princes," the Queen began.

"I don't think you ever asked me for my news," said Jake. "And now, if you'll excuse us, we'll be going. I've waited these two months for Bill, and a dratted long time he took to get here. Told him my address when we were parrots together, before all this happened, and a nasty time I've had, wondering if he'd forgotten it. But I needn't have worried. Slow but sure is old Bill," she patted his shoulder, "aren't you, ducks?"

"But—" said the Queen.

"Think I really stayed here all this time learning how to be a lady?" Jake said contemptuously. "I was waiting for Bill. Now we'll be off."

"But—" began the King.

"Don't be crazy," said Jake irritably. "You don't think I could stop and be queen *now* – when all the Court have seen me and Bill dancing like a couple of grasshoppers? You can have those brats—" she nodded towards

Miranda and the Prince, who were suddenly looking hopeful. "Well, so long, folks." She took Bill's hand and they went out.

And now, if you want to know where they are, all you have to do is go to the island where they lived before, and directly over the spot where the treasure was hidden, you will see a neat little pub with a large signboard: *The Pirate's Rest*, and underneath: *By Appointment to Their Majesties*.

Cowboy Jess

Geraldine McCaughrean

Sheriff Sparrow tacked the notice on to the trunk of the big old hickory tree. It said:

WANTED
Red-neck Pete, for horse rustling.
$50 Reward.

He nailed it right alongside another notice on the tree:

WANTED
Cowhands. Dollar a day and keep.
Apply Lazy J Ranch.

The Sheriff stood back to see if his notice was straight.

"I'm going after that money," said Herbert

from the bank, and he fetched his horse from the livery stable and bought beans from the grocery store, for his journey.

"Fifty bucks, eh?" said Pat Bodger from the saloon bar, and he crammed on his hat, drank two fingers of rye, and mounted up.

"That money's for me," said Regan, checking both his guns were fully loaded.

They peered hard at the picture on the Sheriff's poster, a black-haired, thin-faced man with a moustache perched on his lip thin as a stem of liquorice. Then they rode out of town three different ways.

Jess Ford stood looking at the tree. "I'm going after that money," he said, and walked out of Sundown, all the way to the Lazy J Ranch.

"I've come after the job, sir," he told the ramrod, the foreman in charge of the ranch hands.

"Where's your horse, son?" asked the ramrod, polishing a bridle in his lap.

"Don't have a horse, sir, but I reckon if I work hard and save . . ."

"Never heard of a cowboy without a horse,"

WANTED

Red-neck Pete,
for horse rustling
$50 Reward

said the ramrod. "Never heard of one, and I'm not about to hire one. Sorry, son."

Jess bit his lip and pushed his thumbs deeper into his belt. "But I have to be a cowboy. I never wanted anything else."

"You don't want the cows stomping on you. So go home. A cowboy needs a horse. Go home." Jess turned to go, his shoulders drooping, head down. The ramrod's blue eyes watched him out of a face wrinkled like leather. He was a hard man, but his heart was as soft as saddle soap. "Think you can feed some chickens and a hog or two?" he called after Jess.

"Sure!"

"Caint pay a dollar a day, but you could have your keep, and a bed in the bunkhouse. The hands might teach you a bit about working horses and cattle."

"That would be swell!" cried Jess, and shook the man's hand before he could change his mind.

So Jess Ford went to work at the Lazy J Ranch. In the morning he fed the chickens, hunted out the eggs they laid, and took them to the cookhouse.

"That boy has a nose for eggs," said the cook. "He can find them even in the dangdest places."

Jess fed the pigs and scratched their backs with a stick, then he swept the yard, weeded the farmhouse garden and oiled the wheels of the buggy. He changed the hay in the bunkhouse and shook out the blankets. Sometimes the rancher, Bossman J, gave him notices to paint – KEEP OFF: PRIVATE PROPERTY or NO TRESPASSING – because Jess had been to school and could read and write.

"Danged if that boy don't spell better than I do," said Bossman J.

When the cowhands rode in weary at suppertime, they let Jess unsaddle and water their horses. Sometimes they even let him practise with their lariat ropes, lassoing the fence post. If he got up early he could go and hang over the stable door talking to Bossman J's own saddle horses – the palomino and the grey. Everyone knew Bossman J rode and bred the best saddle horses in the county.

He got no pay. After a week, he was not one cent richer. Jess did not see how he would ever save up to get himself a horse. But he was happy at the Lazy J. When he bedded down at night on the straw bales, and the cowboys were snoring all around, he could shut his eyes and feel like one of them.

Meanwhile, Herbert from the bank was out looking for Red-neck Pete, the horsethief. With that fifty dollar reward he could ask Minnie Good to marry him.

He rode up to Deadend Canyon; he figured that was a good place to hide stolen horses.

The canyon was so deep that the sun never shone on its scrubby floor. There were dark cracks in the cliffs, high, thin waterfalls and half-a-hundred caves. Herbert had a little silver pocket pistol with him. Minnie had loaned it to him. He checked that the gun was loaded and climbed to the mouth of the nearest cave. He could hear something moving about inside! But it was very dark. So he struck a match against a rock. A big shadow leapt up the cave wall – the shadow of a man!

Herbert was so scared by his own shadow that he clenched both fists tight. The match burned him, and the little pocket pistol went off. The bang rang through the cave so loud that Herbert thought his ears would drop off. Then a shape came at him out of the dark.

A big old bear, alarmed by the noise, came wading out of the dark. Herbert threw his gun at its nose and ran. He ran till both heels fell off his new cowboy boots. He startled his horse, and she bolted. Herbert hung on to her tail all the way to the brink of the canyon.

Back in Sundown, at the Silver Dollar

Saloon, Herbert ordered three glasses of rye and drank them straight down.

"Well? Did you ketch Red-neck Pete?" asked the bartender.

"I had him! I cornered him up at Deadend Canyon. *Stop right there*, I told him, *or I'll blast you!*"

"Oh Herbert, did you really?" cried Minnie.

"But he came out shooting, and a lucky bullet knocked the pistol out of my hand. Then the cave roof fell in on him and blocked the entrance. There was nothing I could do but head back home."

"You mean you lost my gun?" said Minnie.

"What about the horses? Did you see my stolen horses?" said Bossman J.

"What happened to your boots?" asked the bartender.

"Herbert! You've been drinking!" said Minnie. "I can smell it!" Then she flounced out of the saloon.

Pat Bodger went up to the old abandoned silver mine. He figured that was a good place to hide stolen horses. He took a bottle of whisky with him, to pass the time, and he settled down to watch the mine entrance. He rested his rifle on a rock and looked along its sights. The moment Red-neck Pete showed himself – PYOW! Pat would collect the reward. He could not see any horses: perhaps they were hidden in the mine too.

The sun was hot. Pat had a drink, then he had another. The whisky made him thirsty, so he had a third. Red-neck Pete did not come out of the cave all morning. Pat tilted his hat forward to rest his poor eyes from the glare . . .

When he woke up, three hours later, there was a rattlesnake coiled up on his chest. His bottle of rye had fallen over, and the snake was drinking the spill, licking it up with a flickering tongue. Pat lay very, *very* still. It seemed like he lay still for a winter and two Christmasses. Finally, the snake stopped sipping. It had no eyelids; how could he tell if it was asleep? At last it fell off his chest, with a noise like a baby dropping its rattle. Its coils fell, *flop*, *flop*, across his rifle.

Pat crawled away so carefully that he wore the knees out of his trousers. He crawled right under his horse, and she trod on him. Then he rode like calamity for the far horizon.

Back at the Silver Dollar Saloon, he asked for a glass of water and a damp cloth to put on his aching head.

"Well? Did you ketch Red-neck Pete?" asked the bartender.

"I had him in my sights. Indeed I did! *Put your hands in the air and step forwards real slow*, I said. Then the mouth of the mine suddenly collapsed – those timbers must be rotten as rotten – and all I could see was a cloud of dust."

"Seems like we had an earthquake hereabouts today," said the bartender. "And to think I never noticed it."

"What about the horses? Did you see my stolen horses?" asked Bossman J.

"What happened to your trousers?" said Belle, the dancer.

"Where's your rifle?" asked the Sheriff.

Before Pat could answer, the saloon doors flapped, and in came Regan with his hat on back to front.

"Well, did *you* ketch Red-neck Peter?" asked the bartender.

"I did! I would have! I had him tied up and slung over his saddle, and I was bringing him in! But his whole gang jumped me. There must have been twenty of them, and they came at me guns blazing. I tried to fight them off, but there were just too many. I had to let Pete's horse go in the end, to save my skin."

"Did you happen to see my stolen horses?" asked Bossman J.

"Er . . . They ran off," said Regan hurriedly, turning rather red.

"In the earthquake, I suppose," muttered the bartender under his breath.

"What does it mean, sir?" asked Jess, wiping his paintbrush on a rag. *KEEP OUT – LOCO BRONCO*, said the notice at his feet. "What does 'loco bronco' mean?"

"It means, boy, that I spent a whole hatful of money buying me a horse, and the brute turns out to be a killer. A black mare. She looks as pretty as the Rocky Mountains – she's about as tall – and she runs like a river.

But she's plumb star-gazing mad. I was robbed. She won't carry a rider, won't even carry a saddle. And she's dangerous. I've shut her up in the dark. But if I can't break her spirit, I'll just have to shoot her. She's a demon, and that's a fact. Now you fix that notice to the loose-box door, so no one goes near and get hurt. Then you can muck out the stable. Mrs J and I are going to town."

There was no noise from the loose-box, as Jess nailed up the notice: *KEEP OUT – LOCO BRONCO*. As tall and pretty as the Rocky Mountains? He just had to see. Jess loved horses better than Sundays. So he waited till the rancher and his wife had driven away in the buggy. Then he shot the bolt on the loose-box door and opened it just a crack.

The sun stabbed the inner dark like a sword. It shone in the eyes of the horse inside. Her eyes rolled, her nostrils flared, and she leapt at the door, baring her teeth. When Jess pushed the door shut, in the nick of time, the horse threw out her heels and kicked at the back wall till it seemed the whole building would fall apart. Planks splintered. The wet new notice fell off the door, its fresh paint face down in the dirt. The pigs started squealing. The hens scuttled into the barn.

Sick with sorrow, Jess tried to get on with his work. He picked up the rake and went to the stable, to drag the dirty straw out into the yard. But he found the door of the grey horse's stall was already open. A man stood beside the grey, his hand on its bridle: a black-haired, thin-faced man in a red bandanna, with a moustache like a stem of liquorice. As Jess entered, the man half drew a gun from under the flap of his long cloth jacket.

They looked at one another across the shifting back of the restless mare.

"Guess you've come to see Bossman J," said Jess.

The man looked puzzled, flustered, then his face brightened. "Yeah! Sure! That's it."

"He'll be back pretty soon. I expect you came about the horses."

"What horses?" said the man. "Yeah. Yeah. About the horses."

"Bossman said he was thinking of selling,"

said Jess. "You must want to buy."

"That's me. I'm buying. That's me."

"Well, if you take my advice, that's not the best of them, you know. The best is the black."

The man's eyes bulged a little with glee. "Is that a fact? Well, why don't you show me this black. I might be interested." The gun slipped back into its holster. A cunning smirk twisted the mouth beneath the thick black moustache.

Jess led the way. He shot the bolts on the loose-box door and opened it just wide enough for the stranger to slip inside. Then he shut it again. Fast. He picked up the notice lying face down in the dirt. *KEEP OUT – LOCO BRONCO*. He would have to paint it again.

By this time, the stranger was beating on the door with both fists. "Let me out! This horse is trying to kill me! What's the big idea?"

"Throw your gun out under the door, Red-neck Pete," said Jess. "The game's up."

A six-gun came skidding under the door. "Now open up, boy!"

"Throw out your boots, now, Red-neck Pete," said Jess. Angry hooves cracked at the loose-box wall. "And now your trousers."

"You satisfied yet? Let me outa here!"

"I might. If you tell me where the stolen horses are, Red-neck Pete," said Jess coolly.

"On injun land! Blind Canyon! On the reservation! OK? Now, please! This fiend's eaten my jacket!"

As Bossman J drove the buggy into the front yard, his wife gave a shriek and covered her eyes. "J! There's a man with no trousers tied to our porch!"

Jess Ford raised his hat politely to Mrs J. Then he said, "Your stolen horses are in Blind Canyon on the Indian reservation, sir. This here is Red-neck Pete. Ramrod's gone to fetch the Sheriff."

Sheriff Sparrow counted the reward money into Jess's hand. "Forty-eight, forty-nine, fifty." Everyone in the Silver Dollar Saloon clapped and cheered. "And what do you plan doing with such riches, Mr Ford?" he asked.

"I'm fixing to buy a horse, sir," said Jess.

"You should get a fine beast for the money."

But Jess put his head on one side and shrugged in the strangest way.

"Nope. I reckon I must be born to go on foot."

He took the money straight back to the Lazy J, and laid it down in front of Bossman J. "Will that buy the loco bronco, sir?"

Bossman gaped at him. "That'll buy you the best quarterhouse this side of the state line! What do you want with that witch?"

"I can't bear to see her shot, sir," said Jess. I'd sooner turn her loose on the range."

Slowly, coin by coin, Bossman J picked up the shiny dollars. "Well, she's yours now, boy. So you'd best be the one who lets her go. But stand well clear, or she may stomp you into the dirt."

Jess Ford went out to the loose-box and drew back the bolts. "You're free, lady," he whispered, and swung the door wide.

The horse which bolted past him was black as thunderclouds with a streaming silken mane and coal-black tail. She pelted across the yard, through the orchard and jumped a post-and-rail fence. She galloped up the hill, to where a mesquite tree cast a single spiky shadow, and there she reared up and blew through her nostrils, pawing the ground with her hooves. Her ears swivelled, listening to every sound off the open range. Then she trotted a way down the hill, her eyes fixed on Jess.

They met halfway, as a cowboy and his horse should: halfway between the hill and the ranch house. Jess put a hand on her neck and the mare nuzzled his ear.

"What are you going to name her, son?" called Mrs J from the porch.

"Destiny," said Jess. "Because she was always meant to be mine." He sprang lightly on the mare's bare, gleaming back.

"Need a job, cowboy?" called Ramrod, as he and the other cowhands rode in off the range. "Dollar a day and your keep?"

Jess tightened the new red bandanna round his throat and straightened his hat. "Reckon I'm your man," he said.

Telephone Detectives

Margaret Mahy

As he dug among the tough, spreading roots in the bamboo corner, Monty heard something clink against the spade. A moment later he turned up a little black metal box – treasure! – something he had often dreamed of finding. He knew it was treasure, and it crossed his mind that it was funny that he should find treasure this day of all days.

Today was the day of the school picnic. The children of Deepford, in New Zealand, were going over the hills to the beach, for swimming, sandwiches, cakes, lemonade – and a treasure hunt. All the children had gone, except Monty. Monty had watched the buses and the cars go by for a while, and then he had gone round to the back fence because he just could not bear it any longer. He had sat down among the bamboos in the bamboo corner and felt sad, in a hot and angry kind of way.

Monty had chicken-pox. There were a few spots on his face, but mostly they were under his shirt, all itching away like mad. Monty wished he felt really sick, then he wouldn't want to go to a picnic. As it was, apart from the itches, he felt quite well and full of longings – especially for the treasure hunt. Nothing seemed fair. In a horrid way he enjoyed feeling miserable and being angry at the other children who didn't have chicken-pox. He lay on the warm ground under the bamboos and sulked.

But that was awhile ago now, for Monty's thoughts had slowly changed. First he had started thinking that the day was beautiful. Then he had noticed a bird hopping on the lawn. A spider swung on its thread, and a tiny little atom of a grub looped itself madly up a thick bamboo stem. "All those things are going on," thought Monty, "and none of them knows or cares that I'm here feeling sad . . ."

The sight of all these tiny restless creatures, all doing something, had made Monty feel better. He had decided to clean out the bamboo corner for his mother, who was really sorry that he had chicken-pox and couldn't go to the school picnic. It was a plan that he could always change if he found he wasn't enjoying it . . .

So that was how Monty came to find the little black box. He picked it up. It was dirty and rusted round the hinges, but that only made it look older and all the more interesting. Monty sat down on the grass and worked round the lid of the box with a stick until he had loosened it a little.

Then he ran to the workshop and found the oil-can. He worked oil round the hinges and round the edges where he had loosened the rust. At last he felt the lid really move and, after trying again, he wriggled it off. The box was open.

Inside were four lovely big marbles with twisty nets of colour winding through their glass. There was a bear carved out of wood, and a little pocket-knife with a handle that might be made of silver. There was a bit of blue glass worn smooth by the sea and filled with watery sea lights. Last of all there was a necklace . . . a pattern of greeny-blue stones hung on a delicate, dull chain. Monty touched it carefully, and wondered.

He decided to take it to his father.

"Treasure, treasure!" he shouted, running round the house and into the kitchen where his parents were having a quiet cup of tea.

"What have you got there?" his father said, taking up the little box and peering into it curiously. His expression changed as he saw the necklace and as Monty told his story.

"If it wasn't for the necklace, we needn't worry," his father said at last. "But I think it's probably rather valuable. It looks like turquoise, to me . . . turquoises on a silver chain. How on earth did it get there?"

"If we were detectives," Monty said, "we could find out. We could go to the people who lived in this house before us, and ask . . . But we aren't detectives, and I've got chicken-pox."

His father suddenly laughed. "What's the phone for, Monty? It might have been invented just for detectives with chicken-pox. I'll start! I'll ring up Mr Davis. We bought the house from him, and he might be able to tell us something."

Monty waited by the phone as his father rang. He tried to guess from his father's words what Mr Davis was saying. It was nothing interesting. Mr Davis knew nothing about boxes of treasure buried in the garden.

41

Monty's father put down the phone. "He says that the people who lived here while he was letting the house, before we bought it, had only grown-up daughters."

"It's a boy's treasure," said Monty. "All but the necklace."

"I think you're right. Anyway, that family moved down to Victoria. Mr Davis bought the house from a Miss Dunbar. She's dead now," said Monty's father, frowning

"Her sisters are alive, though," said Mother unexpectedly. "Mrs Casely at the Milk Bar is one of them – she might be able to tell us something. She'll be at work this morning."

"Your turn to phone!" said his father, holding out the phone to Mother. "Anyway, you know this Mrs Casely."

Mrs Casely had a booming voice, and Monty could hear it clearly when his mother rang, coming all the way over the wires from the Milk Bar where she had worked for years.

"Turquoises?" she bellowed. "No, no, nothing like that! No! She had some nice pearls once – well, not real ones, you know, but nice – you couldn't tell the difference. But not turquoises! Well, I don't know! We were there from childhood. Maybe if you were to ring Mr Mills – Horatio Mills, that is – he's still alive. He had the house before my father bought it. He's been around since the year dot."

"What does she mean – the year dot?" asked Monty when his mother had put down the phone.

"She means he's lived around here for a long time," said his father. "Listen, Monty, it's your turn to ring. Why should we do all your detective work for you? Let's see, now . . . Mills, H.D. Here's the number. He lives over at Carden now, it seems."

Monty took the phone firmly and dialled the number. He heard the distant phone bell going brrr . . . brrr . . . brrr . . . then a gentle old voice spoke suddenly in his ear. "Hallo?"

"Is that Mr Horatio Mills?" Monty asked.

"Yes!" said the voice, sounding grave and rustly.

Monty told him who he was and where he lived, and explained that they were trying to locate people who had once lived in the house because of something they had found.

"What sort of thing?" asked Mr Horatio Mills.

"It's something I dug up," said Monty cautiously.

"Indeed!" said Mr Mills. "Not a little metal box with marbles in it?"

"And a knife!" said Monty.

"And a turquoise necklace!" said Mr Horatio Mills.

His voice sounded quite firm and brisk all at once. "I'll come across right away."

"You'd better not," said Monty sadly. "Not unless you've had chicken-pox, which is what I've got."

There was a strange sound over the phone: it seemed that Mr Horatio Mills might be laughing.

"I have had it," he said. "Indeed . . . but I'll tell you about that when I see you. I'll drive over now."

It took twenty minutes for Mr Horatio Mills to arrive. He drove up in an old car, very clean and shining. Mr Horatio Mills was rather like his car – very old, but very spruce and well cared for.

He smiled at Monty's parents, and shook hands with Monty. "Mr Monty Forest, I presume?" he said.

Monty nodded. He felt too excited to speak.

The box was on the table. Mr Horatio Mills got out his glasses, polished them and put them on. He examined the box and touched it with his thin old hands. "Yes . . ." he said at last. "This is the box." He picked up the little pocket knife. "This was mine, once."

"I can see it's a most exciting story," said Mother. "Let me pour you a cup of tea, and you can tell us all about Monty's find." She settled old Mr Mills in a sunny chair with a cup of tea before he was allowed to begin his story.

"My father built this house," he began. "At that time there were no other houses on this ridge. It stood in the middle of fields and trees. There was a big tree where the garage is now, and a long garden stretching down the slope. My brothers and I played in that big tree a lot. Our favourite game was pirates. We swarmed up and down its branches like a

troop of monkeys, pretending we were reefing sails and climbing up the rigging. There were three of us – Thomas, Reginald and Horatio – that's me.

"One day Thomas, who was the eldest and made all the plans, decided that he would bury a treasure, and we must find it, we younger ones. We all had to put something into the box, but when we had done this it still looked rather empty, so Thomas did a very naughty thing. He sneaked upstairs to our mother's room and pirated one of her necklaces. It made it seem much more like real pirate treasure, I must admit. Then off he went and hid the box . . . but, as you see, we didn't find it."

"But Thomas would remember where he'd put it," said Monty, puzzled. "Even if you and Reginald couldn't find it – he'd know where it was."

"That's just it!" said Mr Horatio Mills, quite enjoying himself. "He *didn't* remember. We began our search climbing up the big tree. We thought he might have hidden it there. Thomas climbed up with us – and he slipped, and fell. He had what is called concussion. We were all very worried about him for a day or two, but he got better after that. The only thing was . . . he couldn't remember one single thing about the day of his accident. So we just didn't know where he had hidden the treasure, and though we searched and searched, we never found it."

"It was in the bamboo corner under the fence," Monty said.

"So!" said Mr Horatio Mills, and nodded

his head. "The bamboo had just been planted then. And you must remember there was a lot more land and garden to search in those days. How funny that another boy should have found it after all these years! I'll take the necklace back for my little granddaughter, if you don't mind, but I'd like you to have the rest of the treasure, Monty. It isn't a very valuable or exciting treasure, but it is truly old, and it was truly buried and lost."

Monty drew a deep breath. "I think it's a wonderful treasure," he said. "It seems special somehow, because there were boys who buried it all those years ago – just the same sort of treasure I might bury myself, if I had to." He looked round at his mother and father, then back to Mr Horatio Mills. "And it seems funny to think I was sad at missing the school treasure hunt today – and then found another treasure here, all through having chicken-pox! Golly, Mr Mills, I hope you don't catch it!"

Mr Mills smiled. "I don't expect I will. I've already had it. In fact" – and his eyes twinkled behind his glasses – "it was because

Thomas, Reginald and I had chicken-pox that we were at home that sunny day all those years ago when Thomas buried the treasure!"

Mackerel and Chips

Michael Morpurgo

A month ago we were on the Isles of Scilly again for our holidays.

"Make a wish, Leah," said Mrs Pender, who keeps the Bed and Breakfast where we stay. My birthday. Ten years old. I blew out the candles on the cake and cut it slowly, gazing out at the lifeboat in St Mary's Bay, the same lifeboat I could see from my bedroom window every morning, every evening. I wish, I said inside my head, I wish I could go out in the lifeboat, just once.

"Tell, tell," cried Eloise, my little sister, pulling at me. But I told no one.

My present from Mum was a morning of mackerel fishing on *Nemo*, Mr Pender's launch. Mr Pender would take me all on my own.

Like lots of visitors, I'd been out in *Nemo* before. She's one of the open blue and white boats that take you to look at seals off the Eastern Islands, or puffins off Annet. Her engine purred and throbbed as we cleared St Mary's harbour and turned towards St Martin's.

"We'll find mackerel off Great Arthur," said Mr Pender, pushing back his sailor's cap. "Be a bit of a swell out there. You don't get seasick, do you?"

I shook my head and hoped.

I'd been fishing once before and loved it. You could catch wrasse or pollock, but what I was really after was mackerel. My favourite meal in all the world is grilled mackerel and chips, with lashings of tomato sauce.

Mr Pender showed me how to let the line out till I felt it touch the bottom. Then I'd reel it in slowly, to entice the fish. I caught a small pollock, which I unhooked and threw back, and a lot of seaweed. Nothing else. Mr Pender fished beside me. For an hour or more we didn't catch a thing. *Nemo* rolled in the swell, the engine ticking over.

51

"*Nemo* was one of the small ships, y'know," said Mr Pender.

"What d'you mean?" I asked.

"Dunkirk, during the war, when the army was trapped on the beaches in France. Quarter of a million men. They sent over every boat they could find to pick them up. Several out of Scilly. *Nemo* is the only one left.

"My dad went with her. Over two hundred he brought back. Badly wounded, some of them. Sea was rough as hell, s'what my dad said." He looked up at the sky. "Don't much like the look of this weather. Blowing up a bit. We'll fish a few minutes more, and then we'll head home."

The sky above was low and grey and heavy. The sea was whipping the waves into a frenzy all around us.

At that moment I felt a tug on my line and reeled in. Two mackerel! But I couldn't get them off the hook. Mr Pender reached over to help me. The boat lurched violently and we fell together onto the deck. When I got up, he didn't. I turned him over, but his eyes weren't open. I shouted at him. I shook him. There was a red mark on his forehead and blood coming from it. Then the engine stopped and the boat was wallowing, helpless in the waves. When I stood up I saw the rocks of the Eastern Isles looming closer and closer. There was no boat in sight, no one to help. I couldn't work the boat all by myself. I had to wake Mr Pender, I had to.

*

When I turned back to him again there was a man crouching over him, a young man in khaki uniform, his arm in a sling, his head bandaged.

"Don't you worry, girl," he said, smiling up at me. "He'll be all right. Needs a doctor. You cover him up with the tarpaulin, keep him warm. I'll get the engine going. Don't want *Nemo* on the rocks, do we? Not after all she's done, all she's been through. Saved a lot of lives, she did."

The engine would not start at all at first. It just coughed and spluttered.

"Come on, *Nemo*," said the soldier, "get your skates on. Those rocks are looking awful sharp and awful hungry."

Mr Pender still wasn't moving. The engine roared suddenly to life. I looked out. We had our stern to the rocks and were heading out into clear open water.

"Take the helm!" the soldier called beckoning me over. "I'm not much good, not with one arm."

Nemo ploughed through the sea at full throttle, the soldier beside me steadying the wheel with his good hand whenever it needed it. The spray came over the bows and showered us as *Nemo* rode over the crests of the waves and crashed down into the troughs.

"Just like it was at Dunkirk," said the soldier, his head back and laughing in the wind. "We made it then, we'll make it now. Look out for the rocks, girl."

Only when we turned into the shelter of St Mary's harbour and the soldier pulled back the throttle did we stop tossing and turning.

"Beach her by the lifeboat slipway," he said, pointing. "And then we'll get a doctor for Mr Pender."

I steered a course through the anchored yachts as best I could, until *Nemo* ground up on the beach and came to a jolting stop, the engine still ticking over.

There were people running down the beach towards us, shouting at us, then climbing up into the boat. Someone was crouching over Mr Pender. Someone else was on the radio calling for an ambulance.

I tried to tell them what had happened.

"What soldier?" they said. But when I

looked around for the soldier, he was gone.

The doctor examined me in the hospital. I told her about the soldier. I wasn't making much sense, she said. But I'd be fine. I was just a little exhausted, that's all.

"Bravest girl in the world," said Mr Pender later. "Saved the *Nemo*, saved me."

"It was the soldier," I told him; but just like the doctor, he wasn't listening.

I had mackerel and chips that evening and tomato sauce, lashings of it. Eloise pinched most of the chips. Well, she would.

The next day, when the storm had passed, the Scilly lifeboat took us all out on a special trip as a reward – for my bravery, they said. As I passed the Eastern Isles, I made a wish. I wished I could see my soldier again, just once, to thank him. But I never did. Some wishes come true, I suppose. Others don't.

The Playground

Margaret Mahy

Just where the river curled out to meet the sea was the town playground, and next to the playground in a tall cream-coloured house lived Linnet. Every day after school she stood for a while at her window watching the children over the fence, and longing to run out and join them. She could hear the squeak squeak of the swings going up and down, up and down all afternoon. She could see children bending their knees pushing themselves up into the sky. She would think to herself, "Yes, I'll go down now. I won't stop to think about it. I'll run out and have a turn on the slide," but then she would feel her hands getting hot and her stomach shivery, and she knew she was frightened again.

Jim her brother and Alison her sister (who was a year younger than Linnet) were not frightened of the playground. Alison could fly down the slide with her arms held wide, chuckling as she went. Jim would spin on the roundabout until he felt more like a top than a boy, then he would jump off and roll over in the grass shouting with laughter. But when Linnet went on the slide the smooth shiny wood burned the backs of her legs, and she shot off the end so fast she tumbled over and made all the other children laugh. When she went on the roundabout the trees and the sky smudged into one another and she felt sick. Even the swings frightened her and she held their chains so tightly that the links left red marks in her hands.

"Why should I be so scared?" she wondered. "If only I could get onto the swing and swing without thinking about it I'd be all right. Only babies fall off. I wouldn't mind being frightened of lions or wolves but it is terrible to be frightened of swings and seesaws."

Then a strange thing happened. Linnet's

mother forgot to pull the blind down one night. The window was open and a little wind came in smelling of the ropes and tar on the wharf and of the salt sea beyond. Linnet sighed in her sleep and turned over. Then the moon began to set lower in the sky. It found her window and looked in at her. Linnet woke up.

The moonlight made everything quite different and enchanted. The river was pale and smooth and its other bank, the sandspit around which it twisted to find the sea, was absolutely black. The playground which was so noisy and crowded by day was deserted. It looked strange because it was so still and because the red roundabout, the green slide, and the blue swings were all grey in the moonlight. It looked like the ghost of a playground, or a faded clockwork toy waiting for daylight, and happy children to wind it up and set it going again. Linnet heard the town clock strike faintly. Midnight. She thought some of the moon silver must have got into the clock's works because it sounded softer, yet clearer than it did during the day. As she thought this she was startled to see shadows flicker over the face of the moon. "Witches?" she wondered before she had time to tell herself that witches were only make-believe people. Of course it wasn't witches. It was a flock of birds flying inland from the sea.

"They're going to land on the river bank," she thought. "How funny, I didn't know birds could fly at night. I suppose it is because it is such bright moonlight."

They landed and were lost to sight in a moment, but just as she began to look somewhere else a new movement caught her eye and she looked back again. Out from under the trees fringing the riverbank, from the very place where the birds had landed, came children running, bouncing and tumbling: their voices and laughter came to her, faint as chiming clock bells.

Linnet could see their bare feet shaking and crushing the grass, their wild floating hair, and even their mischievous shining eyes. They swarmed all over the playground. The swings began to swing, the seesaws started their up and down, the roundabout began to

spin. The children laughed and played and frolicked while Linnet watched them, longing more than ever before to run out and join in the fun. It wasn't that she was afraid of the playground this time – it was just that she was shy. So she had to be content to stare while all the time the swings swept back and forth loaded with the midnight children, and still more children crowded the roundabout, the seesaw and the bars.

How long she watched Linnet could not say. She fell asleep watching, and woke up with her cheek on the window-sill. The morning playground was quite empty and was bright in its daytime colours once more.

"Was it all dreams?" wondered Linnet blinking over breakfast. "Will they come again tonight?"

"Wake up, stupid," Alison called. "It's time to be off. We'll be late for school."

All day Linnet wondered about the playground and the children playing there by moonlight. She seemed slower and quieter than ever. Jim and Alison teased her calling her Old Dreamy, but Linnet did not tell them what dreams she had.

That night the moon woke Linnet once more and she sat up in a flash, peering out anxiously to see if the midnight children were there. The playground, colourless and strange in its nightdress, was empty, but within a minute Linnet heard the beat of wings in the night. Yes, there were the birds coming in from the sea, landing under the trees and, almost at once, there were the children, moonlit and laughing, running to the playground for their night games. Linnet leaned farther out of her window to watch them, and one of them suddenly saw her and pointed at her. All the children came and stood staring over the fence at her. For a few seconds they just stayed like that, Linnet peering out at them and the midnight children, moonsilver and smiling, looking back at her. Their hair, blown behind them by the wind, was as pale as sea foam. Their eyes were as dark and deep as sea caves and shone like stars.

Then the children began to beckon and wave and jump up and down with their arms half out to her, they began to skip and dance with delight. Linnet slid out of bed, climbed out of the window and over the fence all in her nightgown. The midnight children crowded up to her, caught her and whirled her away.

Linnet thought it was like dancing some strange dance. At one moment she was on the roundabout going round and round and giggling with the other children at the prickly dizzy feeling it gave her, in the next she was sweeping in a follow-my-leader down the slide. Then someone took her hand and she was on the seesaw with a child before her and a child behind and three more on the other end.

Up went the seesaw.

"Oh, I'm flying!" cried Linnet. Down went the seesaw. Bump went Linnet, and she laughed at the unexpected bouncy jolt when the seesaw end hit the rubber tyre beneath it. Then she was on the swing. She had never been so high before. It seemed to Linnet that at any moment the swing was going to break free and fly off on its own, maybe to the land where the midnight children came from. The swing felt like a great black horse plunging through the night, like a tall ship tossing over the green waves.

"Oh," cried Linnet, "it's like having wings." The children laughed with her, waved and smiled, and they swept around in their playground dance, but they didn't speak. Sometimes she heard them singing, but they were always too far away for her to hear the words.

When, suddenly, the midnight children left their games and started to run for the shadow of the trees, Linnet knew that for tonight at least she must go home as well, but she was too excited to feel sad. As she climbed through the window again she heard the beat of wings in the air and saw the birds flying back to sea. She waved to them, but in the next moment they were quite gone, and she and the playground were alone again.

Next day when Alison and Jim set out for the playground Linnet said she was coming too. "Don't come to me if you fall off anything," said Jim scornfully.

Alison was kinder. "I'll help you on the roundabout," she said. "You hang on to me if you feel giddy."

"But I won't feel giddy!" Linnet said, and Alison stared at her, surprised to hear her so confident and happy. However, this was just the beginning of the surprises for Alison and Jim. Linnet went on the roundabout and sat there without hanging on at all. On the swing she went almost as high as the boys, and she sat on the seesaw with her arms folded.

"Gosh, Linnet's getting brave as anything over at the playground," said Jim at tea that night.

"I always knew she had it in her," said Daddy.

The next night, and the next, Linnet climbed out of her window and joined the beckoning children in the silver playground. During the day, these midnight hours seemed like enchanted dreams and not very real. All the same Linnet was happy and excited knowing she had a special secret all to herself. Her eyes sparkled, she laughed a lot and got braver and braver in the playground until all the children stopped what they were doing to watch her.

"Gee, Mum," Alison said, "you should see Linnet. She goes higher on the swing than any of the boys – much higher than Jim. Right up almost over the top."

"I hope you're careful, dear," her mother said.

"I'm all right," Linnet cried. "I'm not the least bit scared."

"Linnet used to be frightened as anything," Alison said, "but now she's braver than anybody else."

Linnet's heart swelled with pride. She could hardly wait until the moon and the tide brought her wonderful laughing night-time companions. She wanted them to admire her and gasp at her as the other children did. They came as they had on other nights, and she scrambled over the fence to join them.

"Look at me!" she shouted, standing on the end of the seesaw and going up and down. The child on the other end laughed and stood up too, but on its hands, not on its feet. It stayed there not over-balancing at all. Linnet slid away as soon as she could and ran over to the swings. She worked herself up higher and higher until she thought she was lost among the stars far far above the playground and the world, all on her own.

"Look at me," she called again. "Look at me."

But the child on the next swing smiled over its shoulder and went higher – just a little higher. Then Linnet lost her temper.

"It's cleverer for me," she shouted,

"because I'm a real live child, but you – you're only a flock of birds."

Suddenly silence fell, the laughter died away, the singers stopped their songs. The swings swung lower, the roundabout turned slower, the seesaws stopped for a moment. Linnet saw all the children's pale faces turn towards her: then, without a sound, they began to run back to the shadow of the trees. Linnet felt cold with sadness. "Don't go," she called. "Please don't go." They did not seem to hear her.

"I'm sorry I said it," she cried after them, her voice sounding very small and thin in the moonlit silent playground. "I didn't mean it." But no – they would not stop even though she pleaded, "Don't go!" yet again. The playground was empty already and she knew she couldn't follow her midnight children. For the last time she spoke to them.

"I'm sorry!" she whispered and, although it was only a whisper, they must have heard because they answered her. Their voices and laughter drifted back happy and friendly saying their own goodbye. The next moment she saw for the last time the birds flying back over the sea to the secret land they came from. Linnet stood alone and barefooted in the playground, the wind pulling at her nightgown. How still and empty it was now. She pushed at a swing and it moved, giving a sad little squeak that echoed all round. There was nothing for Linnet to do but go back to bed.

She was never afraid of the playground again and had lots and lots of happy days there laughing and chattering with her friends. Yet sometimes at night, when the moon rose and looked in at her window, she would wake up and look out at the playground just in case she should see the moon and the tide bringing her a flock of strange night-flying birds, which would turn into children and call her out to play with them. But the playground was always empty, the shining midnight children, with their songs and laughter, were gone for ever.

Odysseus

Geraldine McCaughrean

The war was over at last. At last, after ten long years, the soldiers who had fought in it could sail home. Among them was Odysseus, King of Ithaca. He and his men rowed out to sea on their ship the *Odyssey*, leaving the battlefields far behind them.

There was little room aboard for food and water, but some huge jugs of wine stood in the prow, taken from the defeated enemy. Unfortunately, the first time they tasted it, the men fell asleep over their oars. "A bit too strong," decided Odysseus, watching them snore. Then a storm overtook them and blew them off course – to an island, who knows where?

Odysseus pointed up at a cliff. "I'm sure

those caves up there are inhabited. Let's climb up and ask for directions and a bite to eat. Leave your swords here, and bring a jug of wine, to show we're friendly."

The first cave they came to was huge and smelled of cheese. But nobody was in. A fire burned in one corner. The soldiers sat down and waited. Soon there was a clatter of hoofs on the cliff path, as the island shepherd drove his flock home from the fields to the caves. And what sheep entered the cave! They were as big as cows, with fleeces like snowdrifts.

But the shepherd made his sheep look tiny. He was as big as the wooden horse of Troy, and his hair hung down like creepers. A single eye winked in the centre of his forehead. He rolled a massive boulder across the cave mouth, then turned and saw his visitors.

"Supper!" he roared, in delight. And picking up a man in each paw, he gobbled them down and spat out their belts and sandals.

"Sir! We came to you in peace! How dare you eat my men!" cried Odysseus, more angry than afraid.

"I'm Polyphemus the Cyclops," said the one-eyed giant. "I eat who I want. Who are you?"

"I am O . . . I am called No One – and I demand that you let us go! Why ever did I bring a present to a man like you?"

"Present? Where? Give it! I won't eat you if you give me a present!"

Odysseus pointed out the jug of wine.

Polyphemus chewed off the seal and gulped down the wine. He smacked his lips. "Good stuff, No One. Good stuff."

"So you'll roll back the boulder and let us go?"

"Oh, I wouldn't shay that," slurred the Cyclops, reeling about. "What I meant to shay wash, I won't eat you . . . till morning." And hooting with drunken laughter, he crashed down on his back, fast asleep.

Twelve men pushed against the boulder, but they could not roll it aside.

"We're finished, captain!" they cried.

But Odysseus was busy with the huge shepherd's crook – sharpening the end to a point with his knife. The work took all night.

Towards dawn, the sailors heated the point red-hot in the fire, lifted it to their shoulders . . . and charged! They plunged the crook into the Cyclops' one horrible eye.

Polyphemus woke with a scream that brought his fellow giants running. "Polyphemus, what's wrong? Is there someone in there with you?"

"No One's in here with me!" groaned Polyphemus.

"Are you hurt, then?"

"No One has hurt me!" bellowed Polyphemus.

"Good, good," said the giants outside, and plodded back to their caves. "Perhaps he had a nightmare," they said.

Polyphemus groped about blindly. "Trickery won't save you, No One. You and your men shan't leave this cave alive!"

In the morning he rolled the boulder aside, so that his sheep could run out to the fields and feed. But he himself sat in the doorway, his hands spread to catch any Greek trying to escape.

Quickly, Odysseus told his men to cling on

under the huge, woolly sheep, and although Polyphemus stroked each fleece as it came by him, he did not feel the man hanging on underneath.

So captain and crew escaped. But Odysseus called out as his ship sped past the cliff: "Know this, Polyphemus! It was I, the hero Odysseus, who blinded you! Remember the name!"

The Cyclops picked up boulders and hurled them down, hoping to sink the little boat.

"Remember it? Know this, Odysseus! I am Polyphemus, son of Poseidon the sea god. And I call on my father to destroy you!"

Deep in the ocean, Poseidon heard his son's voice, and his angry storms drove the *Odyssey* even further off course – to a beautiful island carpeted with flowers.

A house stood at the top of the beach. The crew of the *Odyssey* ran up to it, and a woman welcomed them inside. But for some reason, Odysseus hung back. Only after the door was shut did he peep in at the window.

The woman brought each sailor bread, honey and wine. She carried a golden wand, and as she circled the table she rubbed it across their heads.

One by one, the men began to change. Their faces grew whiskery, their noses flat. They dropped the bowls, for their hands were changing into bony hoofs. One by one they rolled out of their chairs . . . because pigs cannnot easily sit up to table.

Pigs! Circe the enchantress had turned them into pigs! Now she drove them out of the back door and into her sties, where many other pigs squealed miserably.

Outside Odysseus searched among the flowers at his feet. He stooped down to pick one particular tiny white flower, put it into his mouth, then went boldly up to the house.

"Come in! So happy to see you!" Circe's voice was as sweet as her face. She brought Odysseus bread, honey and wine. He ate the bread and honey and drank the wine. Then Circe came and stood behind him and rapped him with her golden wand. "Now get to the sty with the rest of the pigs."

"Did you know," said Odysseus, calmly taking a tangle of petals out of his mouth, "that this flower is proof against magic potions?"

Circe struck him again. But she saw that her charms were powerless.

"Odysseus!" she said. (She knew his name: that startled him.) "A fortune-teller once foretold that I would be out-tricked by one Odysseus, King of Ithaca. You are my fate! I lay my magic and my heart at your feet."

"Just turn those pigs back into men," said Odysseus.

Circe ran and thrust her golden wand into each pig's pink ear, and in moments the yard was crowded with shivering men on hands and knees.

"Now will you love me?" Circe begged.

"My wife, Penelope, is waiting for me at home," said Odysseus. But for one whole year he stayed on Circe's islands.

Then one day he went to Circe and said he must leave for home.

"It's such a dangerous voyage!" she sobbed. "You must pass the singing hideous sirens and then the whirlpool Charybdis . . . But if you must go, listen carefully and do exactly as I tell you."

Circe told Odysseus and his men to plug their ears with wax so as not to hear the song of the sirens. But Odysseus was curious to hear the famous singers. After setting sail, he told his men to rope him to the mast. And he did not plug his ears.

As the last knot of rope was tied, a sort of music came floating across the ocean.

"Circe lied. These sirens aren't hideous at all," thought Odysseus when an island came into view. "They're beautiful! Untie me, men, and let me swim over and speak to them!"

But his men could not hear him. The sirens' singing grew sweeter: its loveliness almost burst Odysseus' heart.

"Untie me!" he cried. "You go on, if you like, but I must stay. These ladies need me. Listen! They're calling me! Let me go!"

But his men could not hear him, and as the boat sailed away from the island, the singing grew softer.

"What did you see?" asked Odysseus.

"Vultures with women's heads, perched on a rock," said his friends. "And the bones of a thousand dead sailors."

Then Odysseus knew that Circe had not lied.

He also knew that a worse danger lay ahead: Charybdis.

Charybdis was more than a whirlpool. It was a great sucking mouth in the face of the ocean, in the shadow of a cliff. Twice a day it sucked in everything floating within seven miles of it. Twice a day it spewed out the wreckage. But thanks to Circe's advice, the men of Ithaca raced past Charybdis at the safest time of day and came to no harm at all.

But the sea god Poseidon's revenge was not over. His storm horses drove the *Odyssey* back, back, back, towards that terrible gaping mouth. The soldiers just had time to say goodbye to each other before their ship slipped over the glassy rim. For a moment it hung in mid-air. Odysseus leapt on to the stern, sprang upwards, and caught hold of a little bush growing on the cliff. Down fell his ship and men into the raging whirlpool beneath.

For four aching hours Odysseus clung to that bush, soaked with spray and deafened by roaring water. Then the tide filled Charybdis and stilled the whirling water. Broken pieces of his ship floated to the surface. Odysseus dropped down, clung to a plank of wood, and floated away across the sea.

For nine years Odysseus had to travel the oceans from island to island, until at last he found help and friendship and a ship to carry him home to Ithaca.

Meanwhile Penelope waited patiently for her

husband's return. Each day she watched at the window, but Odysseus did not come.

Others did. Idle, greedy young princes came calling on Penelope. "Odysseus must have drowned on his way home from the war," they said. "Marry one of us instead."

"I will wait a little longer," said Penelope politely.

But as the years passed, the visitors became less charming. "Choose, lady, or we will for you. Ithaca needs a king."

"Very well," said Penelope at last. "Let me weave a wedding veil. When it's finished, I will choose a new husband."

But although Penelope worked all day at her loom, the veil never seemed to be finished. Months passed and it had hardly grown at all. And why? Because every night, while her unwelcome suitors were snoring, Penelope crept out of bed and unpicked her needle-work.

Then one night she was found out. One of the suitors found her at her loom, unpicking the threads by candlelight. "Enough!" he snarled. "Tomorrow you'll choose a husband, like it or not."

The ship bound for Ithaca with Odysseus aboard set sail while Poseidon was dozing. Imagine the sea god's fury when he woke and saw Odysseus, his hated enemy, sleeping safe and sound on an Ithacan beach.

Poseidon punished the ship that had helped Odysseus reach home – seized it and cursed it into stone. There it stands, to this day, a narrow ship of rock with stone rowers bending over stony oars. The seagulls perch on it and shriek.

The day came when Penelope must choose a new husband from among the greedy princes. A great feast was arranged. But the unhappy queen ate none of the food laid in front of her. "If only he had come," she thought.

The suitors crammed their mouths and drank themselves drunk.

Outside in the yard lay an old dog – Odysseus' old hunting dog. He got nothing but kicks and cuffs from the princes. His bones showed through his dull coat, and his eyes were blind. Just then, a ragged old beggar shuffled into the yard and sat down. The dog raised his head and sniffed – and got up and tottered towards the sound of a familiar voice.

"Hello, old friend. You remember me, don't you?" The dog laid his head in the beggar's lap and, content at last, died with his head between loving hands.

The beggar shuffled into the hall where the feast was in progress. At one chair after another he begged a bite of food, a sup of wine. "I'm a poor unfortunate sailor, shipwrecked on these shores. Spare me a little something."

But the suitors drove him away with slaps and kicks. Only Queen Penelope asked him to eat food set in her place. "Somewhere on his journeys my husband, Odysseus, may have asked for help from strangers. I hope he found at least one heart to pity him."

"Odysseus?" jeered the suitors. "He's dead and gone! Choose! It's time for you to choose one of us!" And they thumped the table. "Choose! Choose! Choose!"

"Very well." Penelope spoke with quiet dignity. "You shall compete for my hand. And this is the task I set. Put your axes on the table, head down. See how each one has a thong on its handle? Well, I shall marry the first man who can fire an arrow directly through all those thongs . . . using the dead king's own bow."

The suitors swept the food off the table. They snatched Odysseus' hunting bow off the wall and struggled to string it. But though they grunted and strained, they could not bend the bow.

"Allow me," said the beggar, and bent it as though it were willow, and strung it. The suitors kicked him into a corner.

Then each tried to fire an arrow through the thongs of the axes. They all failed and cursed and argued. The axes tumbled a hundred times.

Penelope got up to leave the hall.

"May I try?" asked the beggar.

"Get away, you filthy creature," said a prince. "This contest is for the hand of a queen!"

"Let him try," said Penelope. "I'd as soon marry a penniless beggar as any one of you." And she closed the door behind her.

But once the beggar had the bow in his hands, he did not take aim on the axes. He leapt on to the table and fired one arrow after another – into the hearts of the suitors.

"Hear this and die!" he shouted. "Odysseus has returned to rid his palace of rats and toads!"

Penelope heard the fighting and thought the suitors must be quarrelling again. At last, silence. Her son came running to find her. "He's outside! He's killed them all, Mother! He's home! After all these years, Father has come home!"

Penelope went down the hall. There stood Odysseus, his disguise thrown off and his face washed. "Welcome, sir," she said rather coldly. "You must be weary. I'll have a bed made up for you."

Odysseus' heart sank. Had Penelope's love died during the twenty years he had been away? "I'd rather sleep in my own bed, lady," he said timidly.

"Very well. I shall have it carried to the east chamber."

A spark twinkled in Odysseus' eye. "How could you move our bed when it's carved out of the very tree which holds up the room of this palace?"

When Penelope heard his words, she fell into Odysseus's arms and kissed him. "I had to be sure it was you. And only you could know about our bed!" she said. "Welcome home, Odysseus!"

Time Slide

Julia Jarman

You might not believe this. I wouldn't if you told me, but I'm going to write it down anyway, everything that happened just now. Then I'll go back to the library and try to work it all out.

Before I begin, there are some things you ought to know. I'm not the imaginative sort for a start. "Mary has no imagination." That's what Mrs Scrogham wrote in my last report. I think it was because I wasn't enthralled when she read us *James and the Giant Peach*. I'm just not into that sort of stuff. Boys flying round in peaches, statues coming to life – and time slips, they leave me cold. I like books about *real* life.

My name's Mary Duke, by the way. I wish I

was called something modern, like Jade – though there are three in my class at Cleator Moor Juniors – but everyone says Mary suits me. My mum chose a sensible name she says, and I am sensible. Mrs Scrogham says I'm *reliable*.

You should also know that Cleator Moor is the most boring place on earth. I know that because I've lived here all my life – in Trumpet Terrace, up the road from the hat factory where my mum works – and because we're doing it in history. Till today only one interesting thing ever happened in Cleator Moor. In fact, till 1841 Cleator Moor was a tiny village in the middle of a moor, with just a few sheep dotted round. Then they started mining the iron ore – and the village became a town with houses and shops and schools and a library. Now the iron's all gone.

I've got new glasses, I should say, and a new hairstyle, bunches, and I'm still getting used to them both. The glasses have got red frames with sparkly bits which I can see sometimes, out of the corner of my eye. So, at first I thought it was the glasses, when I was walking to the library and things seemed a bit weird. It was getting dark and raining a bit and the street lamps were flickering and the houses in Ennerdale Road seemed, well, less solid and square than usual. So I started to tread *lightly* while walking fast as I could. I know that sounds daft, but it is nearly hollow under the streets of Cleator Moor, like a giant Malteser – similar colour come to think of it. There's a *maze* of holes under the streets where the iron mine used to be – and once, in 1954, the ground gave way and the school slid into it. Really! That's the other interesting thing I mentioned. A-*maze*-ing I call it!

Jason Ritson's grandad was there – he was a boy at the time – he said it was magic, a wish come true. His grandad didn't like school. Nor does Jason. He said they were all singing in the hall when a great crack appeared, down the middle. There were boys one side, girls the other, with a gap between them or someone might have got hurt. As it was *a cold stillness descended* his grandad said, as the crack got wider and wider, and everyone gawped. Till someone – Jason says it was his grandad – said, "Let's get out of here!" and miraculously everyone did, just before the ground gave way and the school vanished – Now you see it! Now you don't! With a noise like thunder – in a cloud of orange dust which took *days* to settle.

So that's why I felt relieved when I reached Market Square, and saw the library looking solid and safe enough, with its fancy frill of iron railings. The railings are black with a row of golden lily-spikes along the top. There are fancy railings round everything in Cleator Moor. Anyway, it was exactly 4.15, I remember checking the time from the clock on the roof because the big double doors were closed. That was odd – there was usually one door open. Then, even odder, it stopped raining suddenly, and the words *a cold stillness* came into my head. I tried not to think about it. Instead, I read the blue plaque by the door, the one that says the artist L. S. Lowry came to Cleator Moor for his holidays. Then it started pelting down – and while thinking that I wouldn't come to Cleator

Moor for my holidays if I were a famous artist
– I gave the door a push.

It opened straightaway and there, straight
in front of me – where there was usually a
wall covered with notices – was a tall desk. It
was a tall old-fashioned desk, and at first
I thought that Mrs Harrison-Bowe, the
librarian, had put it there. A year or so ago,
we made our school – the one that was built to
replace the one that collapsed – into a
Victorian school. We all dressed up in old-
fashioned clothes and sat on long benches,
and Mrs Scrogham sat behind a tall desk like
this one. She nearly caned Jason for not
knowing his seven times table! I thought Mrs
Harrison-Bowe had done the same sort of
thing to the library. She did know I was doing
a project on it – I should have said that earlier
– and that I was coming today to get some
more information. Our class were all doing
projects on Cleator Moor. The library was
built in 1906; I knew that already.

I called out, "Mrs Harrison-Bowe!" – half-
expecting her to appear, dressed as an old-
fashioned librarian. I wouldn't have put it past

her. She was ace at acting, really brought books to life by reading them out loud with all the right voices. That's how she got me into reading. Sometimes she even got dressed up, in costumes she borrowed from the publishers.

I wished I could stop feeling nervous though. It was *so* quiet – that was the trouble – like those weird moments in class when everyone stops talking at the same time. I couldn't help glancing at the floor, but there weren't any cracks, well, only the zig-zag pattern of the wooden tiles. But that was another change. The carpet had gone – and so had a lot of the books, all the colourful ones in the children's section. In fact, there was no sign of the children's library at all – no bright book boxes, no posters on the walls, or teddies. Mrs Harrison-Bowe loves teddies, and Paddington and Pooh usually sat on the windowsill, but there were no toys at all. There was no play-bus, either. It was usually full of little kids at this time of day.

Where had she put everything?

Where *was* she?

It was hard to see properly. Even the lights

were different, dim and flickery, and as I went to look for her my footsteps seemed to echo, reminding me of all those tunnels beneath the floor. To take my mind off them, I tried to read the titles of some of the books, but I had to stand on tiptoe to read the ones on the top row – a set of Charles Dickens books in dull blue covers. These shelves were tall and dark. Further down I found a lot of Sherlock Holmes stories by Arthur Conan Doyle, but even they looked boring in matching grey covers. Why did they all look the same?

"Mrs Harrison-Bowe!" I had loads of questions to ask her. Where was she?

"Sss . . ilence in the library!"

I laughed. Mrs Harrison-Bowe sometimes *sang* in the library!

"Sss . . ilence!"

I spun round. It was weird being watched by someone I couldn't see.

"Mrs H . . ."

"Sss . . ilence!"

Then I saw her, behind the tall desk, and I giggled because a *witch* glared down at me. Stony witch eyes, bony witch nose with a pimple on the end, long black clothes. And she had a wig on, she must have. She could never have done her hair like that – in snake-like coils, one over each ear.

When she spoke the pimple wobbled.

"What's it made of?" I think I pointed.

And she swooped like a huge spluttering bat.

Unfortunately it took me several seconds to realize that the splutter wasn't laughter but real rage.

Seconds in which she grabbed one of my bunches.

"Bbb . . ut . . ."

Staggering and sliding, I tried to keep up with my hair, as she dragged me across the wooden floor to the little room next to the children's library.

"Himpident brat! What do you think you're doing in here? I'll get Constable Bull to you I will. He'll clip you round the ear!"

Wrenching open the door she hurled me inside and I heard the key crunch in the lock.

It was dark in the cupboard. In the darkness I thought hard. Mrs Harrison-Bowe was brilliant at acting. Mrs Harrison-Bowe would do anything to bring books to life, even dry old history books. But . . .

I listened.

"This is Miss Clack here, from Cleator Moor library. Get me Constable Bull."

But could Mrs Harrison-Bowe move walls? Course not, nor could she put up new ones.

My first thought had been right. I knew as soon as I walked in – walked *through* the doorway where the wall with the notices on it was now.

Was? Is? Now? Then? I still don't know what words to use.

I found the keyhole and peered through it – into the library, where flickering gas lamps cast a bluish light. I saw the librarian holding an old-fashioned telephone to her snake-ear.

"This is Miss Clack here, from Cleator Moor library. Constable Bull? I have a himpident brat in here."

A man walked in, took off his flat cap, and shook his orange hair. He carried a lamp and a box. A miner's lamp. A bait box. Bait was dinner. I'd seen old brown photos showing such things.

"It be slatherly oot, Miss Clack," he said.

She ignored him.

"Ay, it be pelting doon," he said to no one in particular.

Replacing the phone, she glanced down at him.

"Hands, Mr Duke!"

To my amazement he held them up for inspection.

"Ah've come for *Mary Barton*, by Mrs Gaskell," he said, when she'd nodded for him to lower his hands. "Ah' asked for it last Wednesday."

I could see her bony fingers riffling through the tickets. "But you've not brought back your last book, Mr Duke," she said at last.

Mr Duke!

"I did tha' Miss Clack . . ."

"You did *not*, Mr Duke!" She glared down at him. "The ticket's still here for it."

"Then you must've forgot to tek it oot, Miss Clack."

"I did *not*, Mr Duke!"

Then a fat, red-faced policeman stomped in, in high black boots. He took off his peaked hat and his bald head steamed.

"Where be the himpident brat then, Miss Clack?"

"In the cupboard, Constable Bull. Here's the key."

As he approached, he clapped his white-gloved hands together. Clink. Clink.

Frozen with fear, I couldn't move from the keyhole. I just watched those clinking white hands coming closer and closer, till they covered the hole and it went dark again.

Terrified, I heard the key clunk into the lock.

Heard it grind.

Felt the door opening, knocking me backwards.

Staggering, I felt my head hit something hard, then, huddled in the corner of the cupboard, I waited for the policeman to find me. What would he do? I was gibbering, I know I was.

Then a light came on – a bright electric light – and there was a postman! Not a *police*man, but a *post*man! Postman Pat to be precise!

He took off his head and there was Mrs Harrison-Bowe's much prettier one.

"Mary!" she saw me and jumped. "What are you doing in here?"

She helped me to my feet and I looked out of the door past her – at the red and yellow playbus on the blue carpet, at the dragon poster on the wall, at Paddington Bear and Winnie the Pooh sitting on the windowsill, at the shelves of glossy picture books and the carousel of paperbacks near the story-tapes.

Mrs Harrison-Bowe was propping open the door with a chair.

"I'd have warned you about that door locking, but I never thought you'd come into the office on your own, Mary. Couldn't you wait to look at these things I've got for you?"

She picked up a huge old book. "What do you think this is?"

"The library ledger which shows who took books out?" I said.

"Right!" she said.

I took it from her eagerly. "Now if I was the very first librarian of this library I wouldn't have let you have that . . ."

". . . till you'd inspected my hands," I said, "to see if they were clean enough."

"Yes," she said. "How did you know that?"

She went on, "In fact, I wouldn't have let you into the library at all. Children weren't allowed in then, you know."

I kept quiet.

"Miss Clack, the first librarian, she were a right tartar, the old folk say. She ruled this place with a rod of iron. Made grown men blench. Wouldn't let them have any book they liked, you know. She only let them have what she thought was suitable."

I looked through the ledger. It was a bit disappointing because it didn't give the titles of the books people borrowed, or the dates they borrowed them. It only gave their names and addresses and the date they joined the library.

But there it was, my great great grandad's name.

Fred Duke, 5 Fletcher Street, Cleator Moor. Joined 29th April 1911.

It made me feel all prickly. And when I left the library, the clock outside said 4.30, though my watch said 5.00. There. I've written down exactly what happened. Extraordinary? I call it extra-weird.

PS Miss Senogle, who's the oldest person in Cleator Moor, says Constable Bull used to keep marbles in his glove, so when he did clip you round the ear it really hurt. I think I had a lucky escape!

A Dolphin in the Bay

Diana Noonan

The cry so startled Seb that for a moment he held his breath, and when the wailing again swept across the water, he took a great gulp of air and felt he had swallowed the storm.

He scanned the reef, and there it was, the moving blur, the swaying grey shadow perched mysteriously at the end of the rock bridge. Could it be waiting for him to answer?

He put the recorder to his lips and played six notes as loudly as he could. He paused and immediately there came a reply – one long piercing note that seemed to ride the waves to shore. He played again, the creature keened once more, and then it was a game of call and answer, call and answer, as he walked towards the reef.

The shallow pool guarding the bridge of rock was deeper today. He waded through it, feeling the cool wind against his legs as he climbed onto rock on the other side. The creature was still there, still waiting.

People will take risks, put themselves in danger when they are very determined. Fisherman have been swept off rocks and drowned trying to rescue a tangled line or haul in a great fish. Seb was determined. In spite of the gathering storm and his own fear, in spite of the waves that tumbled and crashed against the rock bridge, he was going to find out, once and for all, what this creature was.

The further he walked onto the reef, the more the moving blur took shape – a smooth, solid, fish-like shape. Now the rock bridge sloped towards the water and low waves foamed and spilled around Seb's feet. But there was no time for caution; he was only four or five metres away now and he could see the dolphin quite clearly – or the part of it that protruded from the water, sleek and grey and gleaming.

He stopped walking and crouched down, and as he did, the dolphin's beak opened and its high-pitched cry filled the air. It was so loud this time that Seb automatically reached to cover his ears, and at the sudden movement the creature wriggled violently, the water around it foamed and in an instant it had disappeared into the sea.

"The recorder," Seb said aloud, and after he had blown a series of high notes, the dolphin appeared again, this time leaping effortlessly from the water alongside the rock bridge and cutting cleanly into the waves. Again and again it did this, sometimes exchanging the smooth dive for a thunderous belly-flop so that spray crashed about it like a wave breaking over rock. Seb was dazed. Had anyone *ever* seen anything like it? He wanted to touch the dolphin, to dive with it, to shoot through the water and swirl as it swirled.

It was moving shorewards. Seb moved with it, but now it stopped diving and instead swam in wide circles, its dorsal fin shark-like

as it ploughed through the water. It was swimming closer and closer to the rock bridge. He *had* to get near to it, to touch it if it would let him.

He took off his glasses and tucked them with the recorder into the zip pocket of the jacket. Then he took the jacket off, stuffing a corner of the sleeve into a narrow crack before the wind could whip it away, and left it lying on the rock.

Tiny mussels and sharp barnacles lined the sea wall of the reef, but Seb barely felt them as he lowered himself down. His toes searched for some hold below water-level, and found it. He was up to his thighs in the sea, and waves sloshing against the rock wall sent spray into his face. Any moment now and he'd climb out, but first, first, he had to touch the dolphin.

Without his glasses, there was little point in looking for it; he would wait and hope it swam up to him before he grew too tired of clinging and had to climb back out.

But waiting took forever. There was no call, no brushing of something solid against his legs, only the sound of the waves crashing around him, and that was growing louder. His arms began to ache. He would have to climb out. He lifted a foot, and as he felt for another hold, a roar, louder than the storm around him, reached his ears. He looked behind as a wall of foam and spray rushed towards him, crashed over his head and shoulders, pulled him from the rock and sucked him into the deeper water.

Seb's first breath was a terrifying gasp that filled his mouth with salt water and sent him coughing and choking and panicking as he fought to bring his head above water for another gulp of air. He was so afraid of being drawn further out into the sea that it was all he could do to stay afloat, and now another wave was on its way, thundering towards the rock bridge. He felt himself lifted. He was moving, moving towards the wall of sharp rocks. He put his hands out, waiting for the impact as the dark blur loomed in front of him. There was nothing he could do to help himself except kick and paddle to turn his face from the danger.

But as he twisted and turned hopelessly in the sea, something soft and solid slid behind his back and held him against the force of the wave as it engulfed him, swept over his head and crashed into the rocks in a tower of spray. And now, as the wave receded, the dolphin was pushing him against the powerful tug and pull of the water, protecting him from the force which otherwise would certainly drag him beyond the reef and into the open sea.

He tried desperately to cling to it, to grab at the dolphin's fin, but it was organizing its own rescue, and now that the freak high waves had gone and the sea was once more low and choppy, it swam beneath him so that he half-floated, half-rested across its back as it guided him towards the rock bridge.

He struggled from the water, and as he lay gasping and crying on the safety of the rock, Seb heard, soaring above the thunder of the waves, the distant wail of the dolphin's wonderful cry echoing across the reef.

Rusty and the River Tortoise

Noël Douglas Evans

"**P**lease let me carry her," Sandy pleaded as they walked up the front steps to the stoep of the house.

"How do you know it's a her?" Gary set the little cage down and peered through the wire.

A huge headless shell peered back at them. As if on cue, this prehistoric-looking little animal's head emerged from its hiding; its huge eyes blinked sorrowfully, almost afraid to venture further.

"Hello, little girl." Sandy put her finger into the cage. "You see, she's pretty like a girl." Almost as an afterthought she added, "Anyway, a boy would be frowning."

Closer inspection of its head revealed a smiling mouth. Gary opened the cage and carefully lifted the tortoise out. He looked into each socket. All its legs and its head had disappeared into the shell.

"I don't know how you can tell whether it's a boy or a girl." He handed the tortoise over to his twin. Her eyes were wide with anticipation, her outstretched hands touching the shell.

"Look, it's so pretty, that's how I can tell,"

and she carried it through to the back garden.

A tree dominated the small enclosed area, and tall bushes created a fence all the way around. Set beside the tree was an ugly, brown mud hut. There was quite a high wall surrounding the hut and there were entrances on both sides. A blue plastic dish had been sunk into the ground and filled with clean, clear water. Straw and lettuce littered the small revolting-looking enclosure. At least, that's what Rusty thought. Now Rusty is a collie, a beautiful pedigree with long golden hair. He guarded his house with pride. Often he would pick up the children's toys around the garden and place them neatly by the door. He hated mess. The garden was so beautiful and he loved to lie on the soft green grass. It was his haven.

At first he had been fascinated as he watched Sandy and Gary make this horrible muddy-looking mess. It was all over his lawn, where he lay in comfort in the mid-afternoon sun. Now he sat with his snout on his paws and eyed Sandy with miserable curiosity as she placed this strange shell object in the mud den.

"What could this be?" Rusty thought to himself when Sandy had finished moving the straw and lettuce about. She whispered noises into the hole at one side of the mud hut and patted Rusty on the head before going inside the house.

He couldn't resist a peek. First round one side and then the other. Nothing! Not a thing. It didn't even smell. Rusty stretched as far as he could without stepping over the wall. Not even a sound! Well something was brought here and it was his responsibility to know everything and everyone that came in and out of his garden. There would be no exceptions!

A little hop over the wall and he was in. He shook his paws involuntarily as bits of mud and straw clung to his long fur. "Ugh," he thought. "This is worse than living in the kitchen," he muttered as he edged towards the ugly mud hole. Rusty sniffed curiously at the water. A few slurps confirmed there was nothing special there. He had begun to lift his head when . . .

"That's mine, I think," came a grunt from inside the hole.

Rusty leapt into the air, landed off balance and swerved into one of the walls, breaking it in two places. Water from the leaking hose went dribbling into the little mud den, creating an almost immediate river path. It went through the den and then out the other side. Rusty recovered quickly and edged around the outside, wiping his paws on the grass as he went around inspecting the damage he had done.

A head appeared at one of the entrances of the shell, a piece of lettuce protruding from its mouth.

"Thanks," it said, "nice welcome that is!"

Rusty was dumbfounded. To any human who doesn't understand, Rusty was making some very strange noises. And for a moment he didn't know himself. He had never seen such an odd-looking creature, and to make matters even worse, a creature that looked like a floating shell. The tortoise emerged, munching half-eaten food, its legs picking their way through the sodden muddy water.

Rusty noticed that straw was stuck all over its patterned shell and he had this irresistible urge to laugh. At first there was a stifled snort from his nose, and then a yelp from his throat. He burst into uncontrollable laughter.

What a sight!

Rusty hadn't laughed like this since the neighbours' cat burnt his behind on the stove trying to pinch his food.

"What's so funny?" the tortoise asked.

Between gulps of air, Rusty answered, "You look like ET in fancy dress." Rusty was absolutely right. For a moment, he looked exactly like ET with his crinkly old head raised out of his shell. Maybe that's where the idea came from. "Maybe I should call you ET," Rusty continued, knowing the tortoise wasn't amused at all.

"Can't," came the reply.

"Why not?"

"Because the name has already been taken!" And as a further thought he added, "You're not very original are you?"

Of course, all this commotion brought the family running out.

"RT, then!" Rusty yelled as he was hauled inside. "I'll call you RT."

"RT?" the tortoise mouthed to himself. "RT. What on earth does that stand for?"

Before he could think any more about his new name he found himself being given a good bath by Sandy while Gary rebuilt the mud wall.

"There's a good girl!" Sandy said softly. "You'll be all clean soon."

"And another thing, I'm not a girl!" RT burped.

The two outside lights came on automatically in the back garden at least half an hour earlier than the street lights. It was like a secret wonderland. There was so much foliage it was strangely magical. Rusty was tied up, his chain was looped up over a pole. He was in disgrace. So upset was he that he hadn't even touched his food. Occasionally he would eye the mud enclosure. What a disaster! Embarrassed in his own home by a stranger.

"Rusty," he said to himself, "ridiculed by a tortoise, how ridiculous!"

"So what does RT actually stand for?" came a voice in the dark.

Rusty said nothing.

"Oh come on, stop sulking, I know it wasn't your fault," he continued.

More silence, just the sound of the chain against the pole.

"River Tortoise," Rusty whispered quickly.

"What?"

"River Tortoise," he retorted too loudly.

"Ah, well at least it's original!"

Unbeknown to Rusty, RT was lying right against the wall. He had tried, unsuccessfully, to climb or break his way out.

"Listen, I'm really hungry. I really can't eat this green stuff all day."

"Well, I can't help you. I'm all tied up right now." Rusty was trying to be funny, of course, but it had backfired . . .

"Oh, that's easy to get out of."

And it was too. It was so simple, in fact, that Rusty couldn't understand why he hadn't thought of it earlier. Picking the thick leather handle up in his mouth, he slowly balanced his way up the pole. Standing on his hind legs, he carefully eased the handle over the top. It made a loud noise, *chink*, and dropped to the ground.

The only trouble was, the other half was still around his neck. On RT's instruction, Rusty dropped the loose end of his chain over the wall and hoisted RT up to the top of the wall. He slid down Rusty's back and on to the ground. Ingenious. He then tugged the chain around Rusty's neck and made it loose.

"Now, shake it off!" RT sounded impatient. "We don't have all night, especially if we want to raid someone's kitchen," he sniggered.

"Perhaps some left-over cheese and cabbage."

"Yuk," thought Rusty, and he carefully picked up RT in his mouth and made for the hidden gap in the bush.

They became good friends as their expeditions became more and more frequent. "Operation Delights" they called it. Their amazing collection of food grew and grew, and was carefully hidden from prying eyes. No one would have ever known about their extraordinary special friendship had it not been for the very element, water, that brought them together in the first place.

It all happened quite suddenly.

The summer rains started early and unexpectedly. A small corrugated iron roof sat at an ungainly angle over RT's home. Four wooden posts held the corners while two planks crisscrossed underneath to keep it from buckling. There was enough space for a small person to crawl in from the raised side. The sun would warm the iron roof during the day and keep the inside warm at night. That was the idea anyway.

When the first drops of rain started, Rusty was taken inside. RT would be warm and dry in his home. At least, that's what they all thought. All night, the noise was ceaseless, and the rain tapped its tune on the roof. Bed was the only place to be. Rusty had his basket and blanket in what everyone thought was his favourite place which was the kitchen. A draught used to blow underneath the back door, and there was an irritating drip from a faulty tap. The fridge always rattled and hummed at odd times during the night. This was definitely not his favourite place!

Things only started to go noticeably wrong as dawn started to break. A huge stream of water had found its way under the door and it had almost covered the kitchen floor. Rusty had been barking furiously in an attempt to alert his sleeping family. But he was more concerned about RT. This wasn't any normal downpour of rain. This was a river.

And that's what they all saw in the back garden. They saw a river, which was quickly beginning to look more like a swamp.

RT's roof was in perfect shape. Nothing seemed to be different until they got closer. There was nothing underneath. No straw, no wall, no lettuce, no RT. Just a muddy river flowing away into the bush. Sandy burst into tears immediately. Rusty and Gary went to look in the undergrowth. Rusty went further, tracing the stream onto the road.

He knew now that his secret hole in the bush had been discovered because they followed him. "Come back, Rusty, come back!" they called out to no avail. But he had to find RT alive or . . . he daren't think of the worst. On the other side of the road, he saw what looked like a shell floating down the river. Rusty barked and they ran. Gary ran alongside and made a grab for it . . . It bobbed underneath the water and sprang out at them.

A football!

It seemed to come alive as it flowed with the ever changing direction of the river rapids. Picking up speed and down the road it went faster than they could run. It came to an abrupt halt when it wedged itself deep and hard into a drainage hole.

"Hey," burbled someone. "Hey, everything's gone black," came a voice from inside the hole.

Rusty heard the sound and went straight for the football – he tried to paw it out.

"Help, I can't see!" It was RT.

Rusty barked furiously and the rest of his family came running. No one could get the ball out of the hole because it was wedged tight.

"Rusty, you'd better hurry, the water's rising in here and I can't move," he gurgled impatiently.

It was exasperating. Pure fear made him do something he would never have done normally. Rusty lunged at the ball and dug deep into the leather with his teeth. His jaw went from one side of the ball and then the other as he growled angrily.

"*Psssst*," came from one side and then the other. "*Pssst*," it sounded even louder as water gushed over Rusty's head.

"What a clever boy!" Sandy squealed. "He has burst the ball."

Rusty tore the ball away and almost spat it out of his mouth. There was RT, wedged between some uneven concrete.

His face said it all: it was about time! They tried to reach him but he was too deep. The hole was too narrow. Rusty could see RT clearly. Light shone like a strip of gold across his face and the top of his shell. His old head with its big soppy eyes floating above the rising water level. Rusty's long snout could almost touch him.

"If I was a turtle, it wouldn't worry me but I've never been underwater before," RT murmured, "and stop panting, you're using

up all the air!"

Rusty looked around, "Where's that light coming from?" he murmured to himself. "There must be a hole above, wait here." He pulled himself out of the hole and jumped up on top of the drain where he thought the hole should be.

"I'll be here," RT gurgled. He always liked to have the last joke.

While the children peered into the drain, Rusty started sniffing around. He found the hole. It was a crack in the ground. The trouble was it was concrete, not earth. He started whining and pawing at the ground.

Looking back, RT couldn't remember much about those last moments, those moments before the earth above him started to crumble. He remembered feeling as though he were witnessing a huge earthquake and the ground was opening up. It seemed as if he was falling into the dungeons of the centre of the world.

For Rusty, it was much more of a panic. Spades and shovels had arrived, but it was an iron bar that pulled the concrete apart. When it was wide enough, Rusty made a dive into the water. There was no sign of RT, but he felt the familiar shell around his nose. It was wedged tight and time was running out. Almost afraid of breaking RT's shell, Rusty pulled hard. At first he thought he had broken it and when he re-emerged with the shell in his mouth there was no sign of life. Eyes peered into the dark sockets.

There was nothing.

Rusty felt a movement before he saw it. Water came spilling out of the headless socket and was shortly followed by RT's smiling face. He looked back up to Rusty.

"You certainly took your time, didn't you!" he smiled. "I was beginning to feel like a real river tortoise and turn into my distant relative the turtle." As an afterthought he said, "Now, there's someone you must meet!" He started to laugh.

Now You See Me, Now You Don't!

Marjorie Darke

I've got a white rosette hanging on my wall that isn't there. The rosette, I mean, not the wall! At least, it is there, but you can't see it. I bet you don't believe me, do you? Nobody does when I tell them. Feel the wallpaper for yourself. Go on, it's under the horsey poster and next to my riding crop hanging on that nail. You're nearly there. A bit more to the left . . .

See!

I'll tell you about it.

The first thing you need to know is that I'm nuts about horses. You probably sussed that out already looking round my room. Posters, pony books, riding hat and boots, crop, the old bridle with the oil rag tucked in the snaffle, those bits of ribbon out of Topaz's tail. Mum says it's a tip, but I like having horsey things lying about. Makes me feel as if I've got a pony of my own. Which I haven't. Well – you can't stable a pony in a tower-block flat five floors up. There aren't any escalators and our lift is much too small. It would all be rather hopeless if it wasn't for Ellen.

Ellen's my cousin and Topaz is her pony. They live on a farm just outside our town. I go and stay with her quite often as we are both pony freaks, so get on together like knife and fork. Aunt Win's great too, and Uncle Sidney's not bad. Dustbin's the only blot. He's Ellen's little brother. His real name is Arnold and he's six. You'll understand the nickname when I tell you that as soon as I got through the farm front door that Gymkhana Saturday morning, he ran at me asking for sweets. I gave him a pony nut, though he still had a doorstop of toast in his hand. He gobbled it and was just asking for another when Ellen came roaring up from the kitchen. Specs slipping. Hedgehog hair. She always travels like a fire engine on the way to a warehouse blaze.

"Hi, Vi!" she said. (That's me – Violet.) "You're late. What happened?"

"Had a puncture," I explained. "Had to mend it."

"Hard cheese." Ellen had thrown off her slippers, seized a pair of old wellies and grabbed my arm, all without stopping. "Come on, there's masses to do. The tack's OK but Topaz is a wreck." She towed me through the kitchen, where Dustbin was polishing off the cat's milk and Aunt Win was ironing the newspaper, hardly giving me time to say "Hi!" before we were out and crossing the yard to the stable.

Topaz was a wreck. Enough mud on her to fill up a fish-pond. She seemed pleased to see me and began chewing my hair as soon as I got close to her. In her way she's as greedy as Dustbin.

Ellen handed me the dandy brush. "You start that side. I'll clean her hooves."

We slogged away, scraping and brushing,

till Topaz shone like a copper kettle. Ellen stood back and admired her.

"Fantastic!"

"Super," I agreed.

"Just needs a rub of hoof oil and she'll win the Best Kept Horse prize easy. Get the bottle for me, Vi. It's on the shelf, I think." She had her back to me.

I rummaged amongst the junk and found a dusty bottle. Unscrewing the cap, I sniffed.

"Pooh, what a pong! Last week's kippered socks! You'll have to hold your nose." I held it out, grinning.

Ellen turned round. Well – I've never seen anyone's face change so much. Her eyes bulged. Her cheeks went rainbow. Her mouth opened and closed like that big carp they've got in a tank at our museum. She wasn't staring at me, she had her eyes glued to the bottle. I looked too.

It hung there, twitching ever so slightly. In my fright I almost dropped it.

There was no hand, no arm, no nothing!

"Holy cow!" I breathed, staring down. All I could see where the rest of me should have been was the dandy brush lying on the stable floor. "Where am I?"

Ellen came close and poked at me.

"Ow!" I said. "That nearly went in my eye."

She let out a big breath. "I was afraid I'd go through. You can't be a ghost, then. But what happened?"

"Dunno, do I?" I snapped. It wasn't her fault, of course, but I felt really weird and that made me cross. My skin tingled, which didn't seem right when it wasn't there. I was thinking terrible things about having to miss the Gymkana and not being able to eat.

"Hey!" Ellen said suddenly. "I can see your knicker elastic and your wellies."

It was true. I was in such a flap I'd not noticed the pink circle stretched around my invisible middle, or my empty wellies. I took a step forward. The wellies moved like magic and the elastic wobbled, with the knot at the back bobbing like a cork at sea. I felt embarrassed, and wished now I'd remembered to sew it neatly when Mum told me.

Ellen had got over her first astonishment, and took the bottle off me. "It must be this.

Let's see if I'm right."

Before I could stop her she'd tipped some oil on to a bit of old rag and was rubbing it over the dandy brush.

Nothing happened, except for smears of dirt on the rag and oil on the brush. I could see she was disappointed.

"What *exactly* did you do?" she asked.

"Sniffed it."

For one awful moment I thought she was going to do the same, then she saw her watch. "Crumbs, we're late. We haven't even changed yet!"

"Not much point in me changing," I said gloomily.

"Oh, don't be daft. Even if you don't bother with anything else you'll need your riding boots and hat for the clear-round jumping."

"How can I do clear-round jumping if I'm see-through?" I demanded.

But she wouldn't listen. "There's no time to argue. Come on!"

I didn't budge. "In wellies and knicker elastic . . . you have to be joking! Besides, if Aunt Win finds out what's happened she'll

129

dose me with castor oil and tuck me up with a hot water bottle. You know how she is."

Ellen did. "OK. You stay with Topaz. Shan't be long."

She wasn't and I changed quickly. It was very odd seeing my clothes appear and disappear all the time. For some reason all the things I put on vanished – except for the elastic. I did think of leaving my knickers off, but as Ellen said – what was the point when there was elastic under my hat as well?

The Gymkana was in a field just beyond the next village. We had to hack there. Ellen on Topaz and me on my bike. Somehow we managed to get away without Aunt Win watching, though we had a near squeak when she came dashing out of the front door after Dustbin, who had nicked a bag of crisps and an apple turnover out of the picnic basket. I'd just got hold of my bike handlegrips. They disappeared immediately, like everything that touched me. I tried not to move – tried even not to breathe, hoping my elastics would blend with the wall and the flowerbed. Luckily she didn't seem to notice. But

Dustbin did. I saw his eyes go big as dinner plates. That kid could see a gnat on a chimney pot! He didn't get a chance to say anything though, because Aunt Win swept him up and went inside.

By this time Ellen and Topaz had come out of the yard and I made her ride behind me all the way to the gate and into the lane, in case anyone happened to glance out of a window. She kept giggling, and said the bike looked so silly with bites out of it where I was sitting and everything – just like something out of a Tom and Jerry cartoon she'd seen on telly, where Tom had been blatted and turned into a ghost.

"Oh, ha ha!" I said, rather sour. I mean, it isn't easy to see the funny side when it's you who's nothing but an empty space.

Ellen said, "Don't be such a drip. Think of all the things you'll be able to do."

I said, "What?"

And she said, "Go in for the competitions without paying."

I hadn't thought of this before, but it didn't seem much of a reward. How could I compete? A horse without a rider doesn't count. I pointed this out, but all she did was go on giggling. I felt so peeved that I pedalled like mad, shooting away from her round the corner . . . and came face to space with another cyclist.

The bloke on the bike swerved and his head nearly twisted back to front as we passed. There was a squeal of brakes and a scraping thud. I glanced back and saw him sitting halfway up the grass verge, underneath his bike. He looked dazed but OK, so I didn't stop, and in a minute Ellen caught up with me.

We were almost there and I was beginning to get really worried about what to do next. I'd been secretly hoping that the effect of smelling that yucky hoof oil would wear off, but so far I wasn't even cellophane thick. Another turn in the lane. Past the farm with the hayrick built like a house and . . .

There we were.

The Gymkana was in full swing. Kids, ponies, parents, and all the people running it were seething over the field. A cotton wool voice was blaring instructions for the next competition through a loudspeaker. I saw some ponies and riders moving towards the starting place, past an ice cream van which stood near the hedge. The old excitement came boiling up and for a moment I forgot about being careful. Getting off my bike, I moved towards the gate where a tweedy woman was sitting at a card table collecting entrance money from the cars. She looked up, staring not at me, but at my bike, upright and alone, which wheeled towards her. Very slowly she blinked twice.

And then, as her eyelids opened up for the

second time, I was back. Don't ask me to tell you how it happened, because I just don't know. One minute I was see-through as windows, the next tubby and solid as Christmas pud. It was just like switching on an electric light – that fast and easy.

I don't know whether the tweedy woman actually saw. What I do know is that she shook her head, then pulled one of those leather brandy flasks from her pocket and emptied it into the grass.

Ellen had got off Topaz and as we went in, she murmured, "Hard cheese!"

I knew she was still thinking about sneaking into the competitions without paying, but who cared about that? It was a pretty daft idea anyway.

The rest of the morning was great. Ellen competed in a sort of slalom, where you weave your pony in and out of some poles. She didn't win, but later she went in for the Musical Sacks and came first. Afterwards I had a go at the Egg and Spoon, but Topaz was bored or something and we were last. Then Aunt Win arrived with Dustbin and we had our picnic. All the time I stayed solid and for once didn't mind my podginess. It was so good to be able to see my knees and my feet and my sausagy hands. There was only one slight panic when we lost Dustbin. We found him in the ice cream van "helping" (that's his word not mine), which meant eating as much free ice cream as he could scrounge.

The afternoon was the high spot for me. Clear-round jumping. The course was arranged in another field leading off the first, and there were seven different sorts of jumps dotted about. I ought to explain that you can have as many tries as you like until you get a clear round. Everyone who does gets a white rosette. Ellen was one of the first to enter. She flew over the first four jumps. The fifth was a natural dip in the ground made into a ditch jump with a marker pole in front and behind. Topaz stopped dead in front of this and Ellen nearly went over her head. She took her back and tried again. This time Topaz jumped easily, but of course it had spoiled the clear round. Ellen was a bit cheesed, but she had the red rosette for the

Musical Sacks, so didn't feel too bad. She could have had another go straight away, but she knew how much I wanted to try and said it was only fair I should have next turn. I thought that was ace – after all, Topaz is her pony.

We let Topaz have a rest while five other people had a go. Then it was my turn.

Topaz and I get on pretty well, considering she isn't my pony and I don't get that much practice. We hadn't done too well in the Egg and Spoon, but somehow as I settled into the

saddle again I had this odd feeling that everything would go just right.

I queued up and paid my 40p, watching the girl in front of me start off. Her pony knocked down two poles one after another, then missed the next jump, did three all right and finally tipped the girl into the brushwood fence.

I can do better than that, I thought, as the judge called, "Next one!"

We were off!

The first jump was a single low pole which we took with inches to spare. Next was another slightly higher pole with a couple of oil drums underneath. Then a tree trunk. Both those we sailed over. Bales of hay followed, and that's where the trouble started. Don't get me wrong, Topaz was jumping like a dream. Hay, the ditch where she'd stopped before, a third pole with boxes in front, finally the brushwood fence – she jumped the lot without even flicking anything with her heels. No . . . it was *me*! As we took off before the hay bales, I vanished! Where I held the reins, where I sat on the

saddle, where I touched Topaz with my legs –
all that had vanished as well. The poor thing
was as full of holes as a paper doily. By the
time we touched down I was back. But I
disappeared as we jumped the ditch. Again I
came back, only to disappear for a third time.
It was like being one of those Christmas fairy
lights popping on and off every second. I felt
dizzy, but there was nothing I could do except
hang on and try remembering everything I'd
learned about how to help your pony jump
properly. I was too busy to see if the judges
had noticed anything.

Of course they had!

As Topaz and I (see-through) came over the
brushwood fence and landed (solid), the
judge at the exit was as white as the rosette in
her hand. I knew we'd had a clear round, so I
rode up to collect it.

She backed away. Eyes like organ stops. Then
she coughed and gasped, "Wait a minute!"

I waited.

The other judges came hurrying up, and as
the exit judge joined them I could hear them
arguing:

". . . clear round. Yes, it was. Definitely."

"But over four of the jumps the pony had no rider. That can't mean a clear round."

"She couldn't have fallen off and remounted, surely?"

"She came over that last fence and *appeared*, I tell you. There's nothing in the rules to cover *that*!"

"But I was on Topaz all the time. Really I was," I burst out, unable to bear it any longer. It would be too mean if they refused to give Topaz and me the rosette we'd earned. "I only went see-through for a second. It happens sometimes."

Then an old bloke in a Sherlock Holmes hat, who seemed to be chief judge, said, "No, there is certainly no rule to cover instant vanishing, but I think no one can say it wasn't a clear round. You have won your rosette!" and he burst into a roar of laughter.

Then came the oddest thing of all. He insisted on tying the rosette round my sleeve, and as he did, it *vanished*! It was there all right. I could feel it. So could Ellen and Aunt Win when they tried. But it's never come back. Not from that day to this. Well – you know, don't you? You felt it. Sometimes I wonder if it did, whether I might vanish again. It hasn't happened so far and I get goose pimples when I think that way.

And my wellies and elastics staying solid all the time? Funny you should ask about that. I don't know the answer really. They were all rubbery things, of course. Dustbin thought of that. He's not a blot *all* the time. Sometimes he can be quite clever.

Ellen and I are still nuts about horses. We go to Gymkanas too. But we never use hoof oil. To tell the truth we've never been able to find the bottle again. We have a sneaky feeling Dustbin knows something about that too, though he won't ever let on. But several of the farm cats have a funny way of just being there all of a sudden . . . and vanishing just as quick!

How to Live Forever

Mary Hoffman

It was some time before I realized we had a ghost. First there was all the business of moving and then the strangeness of living in a really old house. Not that we lived in the whole house of course – we just had the usual sort of unit – but the building was old.

I mean *really* old. It only had four storeys for instance and we were on the ground floor. I'd never lived so close to the ground before, so that was weird for a start.

But my parents have always liked old things and they thought a 'turn of the century' house was a kind of status symbol. It wasn't till much later that I found out it had never been intended as a house, I mean as a place to live.

*

I first saw the ghost outside my sleep-room window one evening as it was getting dark. He wasn't obviously a ghost, not semi-transparent, or glowing or anything. He just looked like an ordinary man, not old but not young, nothing unusual apart from the old-fashioned clothes he wore. And he had nothing on his head, so I could see his face clearly.

It was more his behaviour that was peculiar. He was carrying something under his arm – I couldn't make out what – and he came up to the window and sort of squashed his nose up against it, looking in, as if he couldn't see me. And then he vanished.

I don't mean that I turned my light on and couldn't see him any more, or that he moved quickly away. He just disappeared – there one minute and gone the next, like a wiped computer file.

I don't know why I didn't tell my parents. I suppose because I knew they wouldn't believe me. I wasn't sure I believed myself. So I decided to wait and see if he turned up again, preferably when my parents were around.

I didn't have to wait long. I was networking on the internet with one of my friend-groups, nattering on about moving into this old building, when all of a sudden the image of my netfriend Marcia in California dissolved and was replaced by this weird guy's face.

I froze in mid-sentence. The voice-box, instead of transmitting Marcia's cheerful tones, gave out a sound like a slowed-up speech. I could see the guy's mouth moving so I knew he must have been speaking into his computer, but the reception was awful.

Eventually, I realized he was trying to ask me my name.

"Cruise," I said, but he looked puzzled, so I asked him his.

It sounded like "Mister Beresford." That was weird too. People were only called "Mister" on our History modules. I wondered if it was a first name like "Junior" or "Boss."

This net-talking with a ghost wasn't getting me very far.

"What do you want?" I tried.

"Let me in," said the slow voice. "You must let me in."

"No way!" I said and closed the connection.

I sat in front of the screen and found I was shaking. "Mister Beresford" didn't look frightening in himself, but let him in? Did he think I was crazy, or something? Anyway, he *was* in, in a spooky sort of way, if he could infiltrate the net.

The next day, someone tried to operate the door code and got it wrong. Not on the unit, but on the front door of the building. It set off the automatic alert and a security team came round, but they found nothing. Of course not. If it had been Mister Beresford, he would just have disappeared. And I was pretty sure it was him.

But if he was a ghost, why didn't he just walk through the walls? Straightaway, I wished I hadn't thought that. I kept thinking about it all day and when I went to bed, I knew I was going to have trouble sleeping and, when I *did* manage to drop off, I had awful nightmares about people materializing down the modem.

"What is it, Cruise?" asked my mother, the third time I woke up screaming. "Is something troubling you? Surely you're not still unsettled by the move?"

"I think I may be," I said, still trembling. "We've never lived in an old house before. It spooks me."

"Oh darling," said my mother. "It's just a building. How can old bricks be spooky?"

"I don't know," I said, "but I think we may

have a ghost. I've seen things I can't understand."

My mother frowned. "What *you've* seen is
too many scary videos. I'll have to check the
control chip. Now settle down and go to sleep.
Ghosts indeed! You'd think you were living in
the twentieth century."

So I thought I'd have to cope with this on
my own. I waited till I heard Mum go back
into her room and then got up. I couldn't get
to sleep until I had sorted something out; I
was a wreck. I decided to contact Mister
Beresford myself.

As soon as I logged in, I was deluged with
waiting messages. I hadn't switched the
computer on at all, except to go to school,
since the day the ghost had contacted me on
the internet.

"Cruise," said the computer, "you have two
hundred and five messages. Do you want to
see the list?"

"Yes," I said and ran down the names. One
was Mr B. 'Mr' – that was how they used to
write Mister in the olden days.

"Open message sixty-two," I said, "no visuals." I couldn't cope with seeing Mr B's face.

Dear Bruce, the message read, *I hope that is your name. I couldn't quite catch it. Please don't be afraid. I mean you no harm. But I need to come into the building on the corner of First Avenue and Millennium Street. You are in there, aren't you? There's something I need to do there, so that I can R.I.P. Please reply.*

"Computer," I said, "what does R.I.P. mean?"

"It is an abbreviation of a Latin phrase, Requiescat in Pace. It means Rest in Peace. It was commonly put on stone memorials in the days when dead people were buried in the earth, before cryogenics was common practice."

Latin? Surely Mister Beresford was not *that* old? But R.I.P.-ing sounded a convincingly ghosty sort of thing for him to want to do.

Before I could change my mind, I sent him a quick message saying "Be at the front door at midnight."

147

If I was going to meet a ghost, I was going to do it properly.

At midnight, when my parents were asleep, I crept out of the unit, wedging the door open with my father's outdoor helmet. I had mine on as I opened the front door. Mr Beresford was already there. We both jumped.

"Hello Bruce," he said.

"Hello, Mr Beresford," I said. "My name's Cruise, actually, not Bruce."

"Why have you got that thing on your head?" he asked.

"Because of adjusting from a controlled atmosphere," I answered. The fact that he didn't know and wasn't wearing a helmet himself, was enough to confirm that he came from an earlier time. That and the fact that he was wearing the old-fashioned suit and tie he'd had on the first time I saw him.

He was still carrying something, and now I could see it was a book; another sign that he came from the past. I had seen books before, of course, on History modules and in the Virtual Museum. I'd even held one there and

riffled through the paper pages. It was weird.
But not as weird as Mister Beresford.

I swallowed hard. "Are you a ghost?"

I just came out with it and it sounded
terribly rude, like asking someone if they had
an embarrassing illness, but I couldn't help
it. Mr Beresford looked puzzled.

"I suppose I am." He said thoughtfully.
"Not that I think of it like that. I suppose I
just think 'unfinished business'."

He looked terribly sad, saying that and
clutching his old-fashioned book. Suddenly I
didn't feel scared any more.

"Do you want to come into the unit?" I
asked. I'd have to turn the bioscan off and my
parents would have a fit if they knew I'd
invited an unauthorized and unscreened
person in, but perhaps a dead person
wouldn't count.

Mr Beresford looked round the entrance
hall. "I want to go in that door on the right,"
he said.

"That's our unit," I said patiently. I led him
in, fixed the scanner, closed the door and took
my helmet off.

"Now there," he said, nodding towards the door of my room. We went in and he looked eagerly round. Then he collapsed on the edge of my sleep-section and burst into tears.

I'd never seen a grown-up cry before, and it didn't make a bit of difference that this was a dead one. But I didn't know how to comfort him. I was terrified that if I tried to pat his shoulder, my hand might go through it. But I was really worried that if he carried on sobbing that loudly, one of my parents would come in, thinking I was having another nightmare.

"There, there," I said awkwardly. "Don't cry. I'll help you R.I.P. What is it you have to do?"

But that just made him cry louder.

"I can't do it," he said. "It's all gone. Counter, computer, shelves. Nothing there any more."

"There's the computer," I said. "And I have got shelves. Look!"

I didn't have the faintest idea what he meant.

"You don't understand," he moaned,

shaking his old book. "I must give this back."

"Who to?" I asked. "Isn't it yours?"

The ghost wrung his hands in despair. "No, no, I – stole it."

So now he was a thief as well as a ghost.

"It's a library book," he explained. "I took it out in January 2000 and I should have taken it back three weeks later. But I didn't."

"Why not?"

"I died."

Well, that seemed a pretty good reason to me for not returning a book, but I had the feeling Mr Beresford was not telling the whole truth. He had a shifty expression in his eyes.

"I don't see why that would stop you from R.I.P-ing," I said.

"You wouldn't," he said. "I don't suppose you even *have* libraries any more."

"Yes, of course we do," I said. "Only they aren't in special buildings. The things come to us instead of us going to them, through the computer. You can't forget to return something because you never take it away. I mean you can read anything you like and it's still there in the computer library and anyone else can read it at the same time."

The ghost looked mournful. "Not like my day. You mean you don't have books like these any more?" He held it out to me.

"Not with pages like that," I said, putting out my hand to take it. My hand closed on nothingness. It was a ghost book.

We both looked rather uncomfortable. "Why did you want to bring it here?" I asked to break the tension, as he picked up the dropped book.

"This was the library, of course," said the ghost. "The brand-new library built in 1999, to celebrate the Millennium."

It gave me an odd shiver to think of this building, so valued by my parents for being ancient, as being brand-new.

"The issue counter was right here," said Mr Beresford, looking at my study-carrel.

Something about the way he was clutching the book made me suspicious.

"What book is it?" I asked.

He held it out again, this time with the title facing me. It was *How to Live Forever: the*

Science of Cryogenics.

"Did you really die before you could give it back?" I asked.

The ghost shook his head miserably.

"No. I just hung on to it. I was so fascinated that at first I just didn't notice it was overdue. Then I just didn't want to give it back. And there was the fine."

"Fine?"

"Yes, at the rates they were charging back at the beginning of this century, it soon reached an enormous sum. I couldn't afford to pay. And then of course I really *did* die."

My brain was swirling. *Had* he been cryogenically frozen? I tried to remember from my Science modules when the process had become standard.

"If you don't mind my asking," I said, "when exactly did you die?"

"2020," said Mr Beresford reluctantly. It took a moment for realization to dawn.

"2020? But you said you took the book out in 2000! That means it was—"

". . . twenty years overdue. Yes, I know. I told you the fine was enormous."

Something was nagging at my brain. If the book the ghost was holding was a ghost book, what had happened to the real one?

I asked Mr Beresford and he was stunned.

"I – I – don't know! All I know is that I seem to have been wandering round in a fog for a long time with this book in my hand feeling guilty. Everything takes longer when you're dead you know, even making up your mind to do something. And as for getting where you want to be . . . Well, I don't know how long it is since I died, but it's fairly recently that I found the old library building. And now it's all different and I'll never be able to make amends."

I tried to keep him on the subject.

"But what do you think happened to your things? Did you have a family?"

"Yes," said the ghost, beginning to weep again, but softly this time. "I had a lovely wife, very much younger than me and a baby girl. That's why I was so interested in this deep-freezing business. I thought I might be reunited with them later. But twenty years on, my baby girl had grown up and left home and the scientists still hadn't cracked the freezing."

"But wouldn't your wife have found the library book?" I asked.

The ghost looked at me, first as if I was mad, and then as if I was a genius.

"That's right!" he said excitedly. "She would have found it and taken it back! She was a very tidy woman." His face fell. "Then why have I still got it?"

I shrugged. It seemed a funny thing to make such a fuss about. I thought ghosts were supposed to haunt the scenes of their old crimes, like bloody murders and so on, not moan eerily about unreturned library books. Still, I could see it mattered to him. He'd talked about "unfinished business". Probably the real book *had* been taken back; it was just his guilty conscience making him still have it. I turned the full force of my brain power on to his problem.

"Look," I said. "If you'd return a real book to a real library, where would you return a ghost book?"

"A ghost library," said Mr Beresford

promptly. "But isn't that what this is?" he asked, looking round my room.

"Not quite," I said. "I'm not sure that buildings can *have* ghosts. But if they can, we've got to do something to make this one's ghost come back."

The two of us sat on the bed and closed our eyes. Mr Beresford described in great detail how my room used to look when it had been a library, until I could see it in my mind's eye. At last, I opened my eyes . . . and I could still see it!

The lines of my sleep-section and shelves and carrel had gone all faint and blurry and through them I could see a large space with shelves full of the kind of book Mr Beresford had been holding. It was bigger than my room and one of my walls seemed to have dissolved.

The ghost stood open-mouthed looking round the deserted library. I suppose it was the middle of the night in the ghost library too. He walked over to a long bookshelf and found a gap. Carefully he slid the book, *How to Live Forever*, into the gap. There was an unearthly sigh, like a whole forest of trees rustling their leaves. Then the ghost library started to waver and my room seemed to thicken.

Just before he disappeared forever, Mr Beresford turned and waved at me. He looked blissfully happy.

"Rest in peace," I whispered.

I do hope he does. It sounds a lot nicer than living forever.

Hostage

Malorie Blackman

When I left school after my detention, it was already beginning to get dark. Zipping up my anorak right to my chin, I wondered what to do next. I wasn't going back to our house, that was for sure. Kicking through the snow surrounding my wellies, I decided to go to the precinct. Yeah! A trip to the precinct for an ice cream and then maybe the cinema meant that I could put off seeing Dad. I didn't want to see him at all – not after the blazing row we'd had that morning before I left for school.

I hated our house – I never called it home. Now that Mum had gone, it was always so lonely, so desperately quiet. Even when Dad and I were together, we never seemed to have much to say to each other.

I dug into my pockets. A couple of safety pins, a cracked mirror, chewing gum, an unused plaster, my comb, the end of a pencil, my front door keys – but not much money. So much for the cinema! Just an ice cream then.

"Angela? Angela Henshaw?"

At the sound of my name, I turned my head. A woman with dark brown hair tied back in a pony-tail smiled at me from behind the wheel of a dark-coloured Rover. I was sure I'd never seen her before, so how did she know my name? Her car crawled along at a snail's pace as she kept up with me. I stopped walking. She stopped the car, although the engine was still running.

"Angela Henshaw?" she said again.

"Yeah?" I replied suspiciously, backing away from her.

From nowhere, a warm, rough hand that smelt of paraffin clamped over my mouth and an arm braced around my waist like a vice. Before I could even blink, I was lifted off my feet. Somewhere above and behind me I could hear a man's voice, but I couldn't make out what he was saying over the sound of my heart slamming against my ribs. By the time I thought to struggle and kick, I'd been bundled into the car and, with a screech of brakes, it went tearing down the road.

It all happened so quickly.

I looked around, my head jerking like a puppet's. A blond man in a light grey raincoat sat on my right; a bald man in a navy-blue leather jacket sat on my left. I was jammed between them so tightly, I felt like toothpaste being squeezed out of a tube.

Terrified, I opened my mouth and *screamed*. Just as loud as I could. But I got out about three seconds' worth before the bald man clamped his hand over my mouth.

"Shut up! SHUT UP!" he hissed at me.

His breath reeked of garlic. From the smell of his hand, he was the same man who'd grabbed me off the pavement. I tried to scream through his fingers but the air rushed back into my throat, making me cough.

"Listen to me," said Baldy. "We're not going to hurt you. We just want to make sure that your dad does what we want. As soon as he

does, we'll let you go and tell him where to pick you up. D'you understand?"

I didn't answer. I *couldn't* answer. The way my stomach was churning, if I opened my mouth I'd be sick all over my trousers.

"Don't scream again, not unless you want to seriously cheese me off," said the other man, the blond, his ice-blue eyes giving me frostbite. Baldy began to slowly remove his fingers from over my mouth. I opened my mouth to scream again. I didn't even get out one second's worth this time. Baldy's fingers were back over my mouth.

"Right. If that's the way you want it," he said glaring at me.

His hand over my mouth was pressing down so hard, it hurt. His thick fingers covered almost all of my nostrils as well as my mouth. I couldn't breathe. My lungs were going to burst. I tried pulling at his fingers with both of my hands but he just clamped down harder. I looked up at him, my eyes stinging with tears. He frowned down at me, then relaxed his grip slightly. I tilted my head back, dragging air down into my lungs. I wanted to scream and shout and throw myself at the car doors. I had a tight feeling in my stomach and a tighter feeling in my chest.

Don't panic . . . keep calm . . . think . . . The words filled my head as I tried – unsuccessfully – to stop myself from shaking like a leaf. I forced myself to take one deep breath, then another and another.

What should I do?

"That's better, Angela," said Baldy softly. "Just do as we say and we'll all be better off."

"Literally!" laughed the blond man. A smug, vicious laugh that sent an icy chill trickling down my spine.

I looked out of the windows, ready to launch myself at one of the car doors to attract someone's attention the moment an opportunity arose, but the driver obviously knew Deansea very well. She kept to the back streets where there were very few people and no traffic lights around.

What should I do?

Baldy had spoken of Dad doing something they wanted. Was that why they'd grabbed me? It had to be. Dad was the manager of the best jewellery shop in our small town. I'd always reckoned that Dad chose the jewellery shop when he left the army, because it was one of the few shops in Deansea where he wouldn't be bothered with children day in, day out. Dad never did like children. Not even me.

The car jolted, bringing me back to the present and my predicament. My heart was still hammering, hammering, and there was the strangest taste in my mouth. Several moments passed before I realized just what the strange taste might be. *Fear.*

We finally left Deansea by the old Church Road.

"Blindfold her!" the woman commanded.

The blond man retrieved what looked like a lady's scarf from behind him. It was covered in purple and red and burgundy swirls.

"Do we really have to do that?" frowned Baldy. "We'll be long gone before they find her. What does it matter if she sees where we're going?"

The woman glanced around to glare at him. Then she turned to the other man. "Do as I say," she ordered, before turning back to the road.

"No! NO!" I screamed.

I couldn't help it. I freaked. No way was I going to let them blindfold me without even putting up a fight. I kicked and hit out at the blond man as hard as I could. Baldy grabbed me by the arms and tried to pull me away from his friend. The blond man tried to get the blindfold over my eyes anyway, so the moment one of his hands came within range I bit down – *hard*. He swore fluently, then grabbed me away from Baldy and shook me over and over again.

"Do that one more time and I'll make sure your dad never sees you again. At least, not in one piece. D'you understand?" he hissed.

I didn't answer.

"D'YOU UNDERSTAND?" he shouted.

I nodded, terrified.

"Good. Now keep still," he said.

I couldn't have moved then, even if my life depended on it. I remembered how just a few minutes ago – or was it hours? – I'd not wanted to go home because I didn't want to see Dad. Now I wondered if I'd ever see him again.

They had to be after Dad's jewels. There was no other explanation. But there was one big question. Would Dad really hand over all his precious jewels just for me? After our blazing row that morning, I really doubted it. And it wasn't just this morning. It seemed like ever since Mum left, Dad and I had done nothing *but* quarrel.

I'm not beaten yet, not by any means, I thought desperately.

I leaned back against the seat, feeling the double knot used to secure the blindfold digging into the back of my head.

"Don't panic," I mouthed silently. "Don't panic and stay alert."

But it was hard, when all I wanted to do was cry and never stop. My heart was still bouncing about in my chest and my stomach was turning over like a tumble-drier.

If you're going to be sick, do it over one of them – not over yourself, I thought.

The first thing to do was to get my bearings. I sat still between the two men and tried to think rationally. I tilted my head up slightly but I couldn't see under the blindfold. I lowered my head again. Now what?

Well . . . we'd left Deansea by the old Church Road, and since they'd blindfolded me, we'd been travelling for at least three minutes. How fast? Not as fast as my dad when he drove, so less than forty miles an hour? I couldn't be sure.

I started to count. When I'd reached six hundred, the car turned left. I started counting from one again – slow and steady, counting off the seconds. It was a trick Dad had been taught in the army. The only time we didn't seem to argue was when he was reminiscing about the army.

I carried on counting. The road wound around a bit but the car didn't slow down to make a proper turn until I reached one thousand four hundred, then it turned right. I counted to one hundred and twenty before the car turned right again. We must have turned on to a track or a field because the car – and everyone in it – bounced up and down as if we were all on a trampoline.

167

And all the time, no one in the car said a word. I tried to memorize the route we were taking, like memorizing the numbers to open a safe. Six hundred left, fourteen hundred right, one hundred and twenty right. Abruptly the car stopped and the engine was turned off. I looked around as if to see through the scarf covering my eyes. I heard the driver's door open, followed by both the doors at the back. I sat still, listening to my kidnappers get out of the car.

"This way."

My left arm was grabbed by Baldy and I was pulled out of the car. The snow was fresher here than in town. It crunched under my wellies. I heard the wind whistling in some tall trees to my right. We turned to the left and started walking. After ten steps the ground became firm as we entered some kind of house. I heard a door shut behind me. I'd never been so frightened by the sound of a door closing before.

After five steps, Baldy said gruffly, "Stairs!"

I lifted my feet higher and started climbing

up some steps. I counted twelve in all, the fifth one being the most creaky.

Suddenly I couldn't stop counting.

At the top of the stairs I was led into another room. I stood still.

"C-Can I t-take my blindfold off n-now?" I whispered, my hands moving up towards my eyes.

No one tried to stop me so I pulled the blindfold off my face, blinking rapidly to focus. The room I was in was sombre, with blue painted walls and a wooden floor. Apart from the chair beside me, the only other piece of furniture was a table with a newspaper and a squashed lager can on it. Out of the corner of my eye I saw that the window had had planks of wood nailed across it. My kidnappers watched me. The silence in the room was deafening.

"W-What d'you want my dad to do?" I squeaked, more to hear myself speak than for any other reason, because I'd already guessed what they were after. But if I could speak then I was alive. And if I was alive, then I could get out of this. I *could.*

The two men regarded each other over my head.

"Let's just say, we want him to make a delivery," said the blond.

"And he'd better not mess us about either," said Baldy.

"A de-delivery . . .?" I stammered.

"Yeah!" Baldy grinned. "One that—"

"Shut up, Quill!" the blond man snapped harshly.

"We're not supposed to use our names in front of the girl – remember?" the woman driver said quietly.

They all turned to look at me. I couldn't help it – I burst into tears.

What would Dad say if he could see me now . . . ? In the past, whenever I felt like crying, I just had to think about what Dad would say if he caught me and the tears never got past my eyelids, but this time it didn't work. In fact, if anything, thinking of Dad just made me cry more.

If Dad was here instead of you, he wouldn't cry, I told myself. Nothing could ever make Dad cry.

"Tie her hands and legs together," said the woman, after a long pause.

"I'll tie her to the chair," said the blond man, moving forward.

"I'll do it," said Quill.

"Don't you trust me?" snapped the blond man.

I kept my head down, still crying. As long as they were arguing amongst themselves, they wouldn't concentrate on me. The blond man was the one to be most wary of. All he cared about were the jewels from Dad's shop. I didn't matter. I was just a means to an end. And the woman was almost as bad. Only Quill thought of me as a person.

While crying, I wondered if I could or even should make a break for it. I could get past the two men, but the woman was right by the door. The woman walked over to Quill and whispered in his ear. I took a deep breath. It was now or never.

Quill moved forward to stand in front of me and the opportunity to make a break for it slipped away. Would I get another?

"When you've finished, come downstairs,"

said the woman. "I want to talk to you – *both* of you."

The woman and the blond man left the room. I heard them walk downstairs. I turned to my captor.

"Don't tie me up, Quill," I whispered. "I couldn't bear it."

"I've got no choice," he said gruffly. "And I'd forget that name if I were you. Don't use it in front of the others."

I shook my head. I wasn't stupid.

"Are you . . . after the jewels in my Dad's shop? Is that the d-delivery you were all talking about?" I asked.

Quill took some thin, plastic rope out of his jacket pocket before nodding. My heart sunk to my toenails at the sight of it. Dad used the same kind for wrapping parcels at home. It was deceptively thin and very strong – almost unbreakable.

"Once we get the jewels, we'll let you go. I promise," said Quill.

"And if Dad doesn't hand them over?"

"He wants you back, doesn't he?"

The question turned my blood cold –

because that was the problem. *I didn't know*. Dad loved his shop and his jewels. When the quarrels between him and Mum became too bitter, when the atmosphere at home grew too tense, Dad always retreated to his shop. I'll never forget how Mum once sent me to fetch Dad from his "precious hideout" (her words). When I arrived the shop was shut but I could see Dad through the window. For ages I watched him dust the displays of gold and silver necklaces, lovingly polish the gold rings, dust off the expensive gem stones. I actually felt jealous. Then I felt foolish and incredibly angry for being jealous of bits of metal and fancy glass. Still angry, I banged on the shop door so hard, I almost broke the glass. I remember how Dad had shouted at me for that too.

"Come on. This won't take long. Put your hands behind your back," Quill ordered.

Slowly, reluctantly, I did as directed. Then I remembered something Dad had once told me – something else he'd learnt in the army. Keeping my wrists together, I bent my hands back, with my palms as far apart from each other as I could get them. Quill tied my wrists together – tight. I sat down, then he squatted down to tie my ankles. I tried to keep my ankles together and my feet apart, flexing my feet upwards. Dad told me that if someone is tying you up, they'll need more rope to tie your hands and legs if you tense your muscles and flex your hands and feet. That way, when you relaxed, the ropes would be looser than if you simply relaxed to begin with. When Quill had finished he stood up.

"Do I have to gag you?" he asked.

I shook my head quickly. I couldn't bear the thought of something over my mouth.

"One single squeak out of you and I'll muzzle you like a dog. D'you understand?"

I nodded.

"There's no use shouting or screaming, we're miles from the nearest house. All you'll do is make the two downstairs very angry. D'you understand that?" Quill said.

I nodded again. I heard footsteps, then the other two came back into the room. The woman was carrying a cordless phone, the receiver to her ear.

174

"Mr Henshaw, you *will* do exactly as we say . . ." She stopped speaking.

I could hear Dad's furious voice at the other end of the line.

"Listen to me, Mr Henshaw," the woman interrupted, her voice just as angry. "I have someone here who'll persuade you to change your mind. Say hello to your father, Angela."

She thrust the phone against my ear.

"Dad . . ." I whispered. "Dad, is that you?"

"Angela . . . ?" Dad was shocked. "Angela, are you all right?" His voice was scared and angry, all at once.

"Dad, I'm frightened . . ." The receiver was yanked away from me.

"That's enough," said the woman. She and the blond man left the room and started downstairs, all the time talking urgently into the phone.

"Like I said, behave yourself and you'll be home before you know it," said Quill. And with that, he left the room, locking the door behind him. I sat perfectly still with my eyes closed, allowing the seconds to tick by. When I opened my eyes I was still tied up in a room

I'd never seen before. I wasn't dreaming . . .

It was time to do something. I forced myself to relax. Immediately, my bonds felt looser. I stood up, my hands still behind my back. Then I lay down on the cold wooden floor, desperate not to make a sound. Lying on my side, I curled up tightly into a ball until I could slip my tied hands past my hips and over the backs of my legs, slipping my feet, heels first, through the circle made by my arms. It took less than a minute – I'm very supple. Sitting up again, I worked away at the rope binding my feet.

The nylon rope cut into my fingers as I worked to unknot it, but at last it fell away from my ankles. Untying the rope that bound my hands was trickier. I had to use my teeth and the index finger of one hand and the thumb of the other to pry the knot open. But I did it.

Now what?

I stood up and silently moved over to the nailed-up window. That was no good. There was no way I could pull at the boards that covered the window without making some kind of noise that would alert my abductors.

"Don't just act. Think first," I muttered.

Think . . . think . . . think . . . I looked in my pockets, hoping that something in there would give me an idea. I looked around. My mind was still a blank. I tiptoed across to the door. Even though I'd heard Quill turn the key in the lock, I turned the doorknob anyway. Nothing. But then, what did I expect? Putting my eye against the keyhole, I tried to see if one of my kidnappers was on the landing guarding my door, but I couldn't see a thing. The key was still in the lock from outside. I leant my head against the door, forcing my eyes wide open so I wouldn't cry again.

And that's when an idea sneaked into my head. A very dangerous idea . . .

I crept across the room to retrieve the newspaper. Laying it flat, I pushed it through the gap beneath the door, so that the newspaper was half on my side of the door, with the other half on the landing. I shuffled the newspaper so it was directly underneath the key. After putting a stick of chewing gum in my mouth, I straightened out one of the safety pins I had and started poking about in the lock. The key began to shift backwards until it dropped out of the lock, landing with a *clink* on the newspaper. I panicked. Had they heard it downstairs? Quickly I pulled the newspaper through to my side of the door. The door key was there on the newspaper. I froze, expecting to hear my kidnappers rush up the stairs at any moment.

Silence.

Unlocking the door, I opened it fully until it was almost touching the adjacent wall. I chewed harder on my chewing gum. Now came the hardest part of all. I ran over to the window and started banging my fists on the planks nailed across it.

"Help . . . HELP!" I screamed at the top of my lungs.

Immediately I heard footsteps thundering up the stairs.

Please let it be all of them . . . I prayed. I raced across the room to stand behind the door. I wiped my sweaty hands on my coat, grasping the key to me.

"You were supposed to tie her up," the woman said furiously.

"I did," I heard Quill answer.

"The door's wide open," said the blond man.

They all came racing into the room. This was it. I darted around the door and pulled it shut, jamming the key into the lock as I pulled it. My kidnappers shouted at me and I saw the blond man lunge at the door before it closed. Frantically, I turned the key in the lock. Only just in time. The doorknob rattled violently. Quickly taking the chewing gum out of my mouth, I stuffed it into the keyhole, using the end of the pencil I had to push it right in.

"Get out the way. I've got a spare key," I heard the woman say.

For the first time since they'd captured me, I allowed myself a slight smile. I hadn't known for certain that they had a spare key. I'd just thought I'd better play safe. But now the woman's spare key wouldn't do her much good, not with the chewing gum and my pencil in the lock.

"Angela, open this door. NOW!" the blond man demanded.

Yeah, Likely! I thought, and raced down the stairs. I didn't have much time.

There it was – what I'd been looking for. *The telephone* . . .

The others were still shouting and screaming at me from upstairs. The doorknob rattled as they tried to open the door.

I picked up the receiver. Where would Dad be? At home or at his shop? I didn't have time to find out. It would be faster to phone the police. I dialled 999 and asked the emergency operator for the police. Upstairs, they were now trying to batter the door down. At last I was put through.

"Please help me. My name's Angela Henshaw. My dad owns Henshaw's Jewellers in the precinct. Listen! I've been kidnapped. The kidnappers left Deansea by the old Church Road. We drove for about three minutes straight, then six hundred left, fourteen hundred right, one hundred and twenty right. No! Don't interrupt! Ask Dad, he'll tell you what it means!" I rushed on urgently as the voice at the other end tried to cut in. "I've been kidnapped and I don't know where . . ."

But at that moment, the upstairs door splintered. The noise crashed through the house. The next second lasted for ever. It was as if the very air in the house froze. I stood stricken in the hall.

Then everything happened at once. I heard shouting but I was too terrified to make out the words. And then came footsteps running – all over the sound of my heart thundering. I didn't wait to hear any more. Almost blind with panic, I threw myself at the front door. My hands were all thumbs as I frantically pulled at the door latch.

Don't turn around . . . I kept telling myself that over and over, as if by not turning around, I could stop my kidnappers from catching me.

The door opened. It must have taken only a second, two at the most, but that's not how it felt.

"ANGELA . . . !"

"COME BACK HERE . . ."

From somewhere close behind me came the voices of Baldy and the woman.

Don't turn around . . .

Fingers touched my shoulder. I screamed and, head bent, charged towards the moonlit trees as fast as I could, before whoever it was could get a good grip. Then the moon disappeared behind a cloud and I couldn't see my hand in front of my face – but I didn't care. If I had to choose between the dark and the kidnappers, then the dark would win hands down.

"ANGELA . . . COME BACK HERE . . ."

"WE WON'T HURT YOU . . ."

"DAMN IT! COME BACK . . ."

Their voices seemed to come from everywhere at once. I couldn't hear their footsteps – the snow was too deep. For all I knew I might be about to head-butt one of them in the stomach. Good!

Don't look back, Angela. Keep running.

I heard one of the men shouting something about the phone, but I was too panicky to listen properly. I slipped, then clambered up immediately and kept on running. I ran and ran until I thought my lungs would burst like balloons – and still I kept running. I couldn't hear their voices any more. It didn't matter.

Keep running . . .

And then the ground disappeared. I started falling and falling. I thought I'd never stop.

But I didn't scream.

I must have been knocked out, because I woke up as if from a really bad nightmare – the worst nightmare I'd ever had in my life. Except that it was still dark and bitterly cold – and no dream. My head, my whole body, ached. I couldn't see a thing, but I could sense that something wasn't quite right. I shifted around slightly, feeling about with my hands. There was about forty centimetres of solidness in front of me and after that . . . nothing. I was on a long, thin ledge somewhere and goodness only knew how long the drop was beyond that.

What was left of my courage vanished.

"HELP!" I screamed at the top of my voice. I stretched up and shouted again. "HELP!"

The ledge moved. I actually felt it vibrate and slip slightly.

I couldn't breathe. I was choking – choking on terror. Slowly, I felt behind me for a handhold. There was none. I was so cold and it was getting worse. I felt so tired. All I wanted to do was sleep. But I remembered Dad telling me once that if you were stuck outside somewhere and really cold, one of the worst things you could do was give in to it and go to sleep.

"Do that and you might never wake up again," he had said.

I couldn't give up. I *wouldn't*.

Dad . . . If only I could see him one more

time – just to hug him and say . . . sorry.

"DAD . . ." I shouted desperately.

"ANGELA? ANGELA!"

And then there was a light shining in my eyes, dazzling me.

"Angela, hang on. I'm here with the police. You've fallen part of the way down Deansea quarry. Stay still. We're coming down to get you."

I couldn't help it. I started crying again. Sobbing even harder than before. Because it was my dad.

My dad had come to get me.

In the torchlight above, I saw the policeman tie a rope around his waist.

"Angela, I'm Police Sergeant Kent. It's all right. I'm coming to get you, so don't run off, will you!"

That made me laugh a bit, even though I was still crying. Dad and the other policemen and women then held on to the other end of the rope. Sergeant Kent came down for me and lifted me like a sack of potatoes onto his shoulder. Then he climbed back up the quarry face. Dad lifted me off the policeman's back before my feet even touched the ground. I don't know which was tighter – Dad hugging me, or me hugging Dad. My cheek against Dad's was wet, but now I wasn't the one crying. There were three policemen and a policewoman around us, shining torches at us and grinning like Cheshire cats.

"Dad, d-did you give the kidnappers your jewels?" I asked in a whisper.

"Angela, I would have given them everything I had to get you back home safely." Dad smiled.

"How did you know where to find me?" I sniffed.

"We got to your father just as he was about to leave his shop with two carrier bags filled with jewels. He was able to decipher your cryptic message for us," said the policeman closest to us.

Dad and I smiled at each other.

"Really, sir, you should have got in touch with us right away," said Sergeant Kent to Dad. "We in the police know how to handle things like this."

"I didn't want to risk it," Dad said. "Angela

means more to me than all the jewels in the world."

"Where are the kidnappers?" I asked.

"We've got them all," said the policewoman. "They still don't understand how you could have told us about their hideaway when you were blindfolded throughout the drive up here!"

"Why don't you two leave now. Our questions can wait until tomorrow," said Sergeant Kent.

"Dad, can we go home?" I whispered.

"I'll cook you your favourite dinner while you have a bath and get warm. Then we'll talk. OK?"

"OK." I grinned. That was all I'd ever wanted.

We walked hand in hand back to Dad's car.

ACKNOWLEDGEMENTS

The publishers wish to thank the following for permission to reproduce copyright material.

Joan Aiken: for "The Parrot Pirate Princess" from *All You Ever Wanted*, Jonathan Cape Ltd, 1953. Copyright © Joan Aiken Enterprises Ltd, by permission of A M Heath & Co Ltd on behalf of the author.

Malorie Blackman: for "Hostage" from *Amazing Adventure Stories*, Doubleday, pp. 25–48. Copyright © 1994 Malorie Blackman, by permission of A M Heath & Co Ltd on behalf of the author.

Marjorie Darke: for "Now You See Me, Now You Don't" from *The Cat-Flap and the Apple Pie,* compiled by L Salway, W H Allen. Copyright © 1979 Marjorie Darke, by permission of Rogers, Coleridge & White Ltd on behalf of the author.

Noel Douglas Evans: for "Rusty and the River Tortoise" from *Animal*, Struik Publishers, 1994, by permission of the author.

Mary Hoffman: for "How to Live Forever" from *Stacks of Stories* ed. Mary Hoffman, 1997, pp. 103–118, by permission of The Library Association.

Julia Jarman: for "Time Slide" from *Stacks of Stories*, ed. Mary Hoffman, 1997, pp. 89–102, by permission of The Library Association.

Margaret Mahy: for "Telephone Detectives" from *The Horrible Stories and Others*, J M Dent, pp. 58–66, by permission of The Orion Publishing Group Ltd.

Geraldine McCaughrean: for "Odysseus" from *The Orchard Book of Greek Myths*, Orchard Books, 1992, pp. 84–94, by permission of The Watts Publishing Group Ltd; and for an extract from *Cowboy Jess* by Geraldine McCaughrean, J M Dent, 1995, pp. 5-19, by permission of The Orion Publishing Group Ltd.

Michael Morpurgo: for "Mackerel and Chips", 1995, by permission of David Higham Associates on behalf of the author.

Diana Noonan: for "A Dolphin in the Bay", Omnibus Books. Copyright © 1993 Diana Noonan, by permission of Scholastic Australia.

Every effort has been made to trace the copyright holders but where this has not been possible or where any error has been made the publishers will be pleased to make the necessary arrangements at the first opportunity.

More top stories can be found in

Scary Stories for Eight Year Olds

Chosen by Helen Paiba

Scary stories include:

The Ghost of Old Man Chompers

The Bones That Came Back to Life

The Blood-thirsty Crocodile

The Girl Who Ate Too Much Chocolate

The Ghost Dogs' Revenge

More top stories can be found in

Funny Stories for Eight Year Olds

Chosen by Helen Paiba

Hilarious stories include:

The Unidentified Flying Dog

The Man Who Couldn't Stop
Laughing

The Amazing Talking Baby

The Boy Who Turned into
a Frog

The Exploding Jelly Custard
Surprise

More top stories can be found in

Animal Stories for Eight Year Olds

Chosen by Helen Paiba

Exciting stories include:

The Circus Pony's Great Escape

How Billy Bear Lost His Tail

Yucky, the Ugly Duckling

The Rabbit Who Tricked a Tiger

Sid the Mosquito's Fantastic
Feast

More top stories can be found in

Funny Stories for Nine Year Olds

Chosen by Helen Paiba

Hilarious stories include:

The Boy Who Turned Himself Green

Miss Pettigrew's Disappearing Parrot

Doctor Bananas, The Magical Laughter-maker

The Night the Bed Fell Down

Reginald, the Reluctant Dragon

More top stories can be found in

Scary Stories for Nine Year Olds

Chosen by Helen Paiba

Scary stories include:

The Ghostly Encounter in a
Graveyard

The Haunted Windmill

The Babysitter's Evil Eye

The Curse of the Sea Bride

Padfoot, the Prowling Ghost Dog

More top stories can be found in

Animal Stories for Nine Year Olds

Chosen by Helen Paiba

Exciting stories include:

The Dog Who Became a
School-teacher

Morocco, the Amazing Magical
Pony

The Upside-down Mice

The Tiger Cub Who Loved
Children

Pally Ali and His Clever Camels

Books in this series available from Macmillan

The prices shown below are correct at the time of going to press. However, Macmillan Publishers reserve the right to show new retail prices on covers which may differ from those previously advertised.

All Pan Macmillan titles can be ordered from our website, www.panmacmillan.com, or from your local bookshop and are available by post from:

Bookpost
PO Box 29, Douglas, Isle of Man IM99 1BQ

Credit cards accepted. For details:
Telephone: 01624 836000
Fax: 01624 670923
E-mail: bookshop@enterprise.net
www.bookpost.co.uk

Free postage and packing in the UK.